The Intersection of Faith and School Leadership

Memoirs of a School Administrator

JAMES FITZPATRICK

To my wife Therese – all my love!

TABLE OF CONTENTS

Part 1:
Growing up Catholic in the Western Suburbs of Chicago

The Intersection of Faith and School Leadership: The Memoirs of a School Administrator

Foreword

When I first learned about *The Intersection of Faith and School Leadership: The Memoirs of a School Administrator*, I immediately thought, "This a very important and timely book." In a world where the pressures on school leaders seem to grow by the day—political polarization, social unrest, funding challenges—the question of how we ground ourselves has never been more relevant. For Jim Fitzpatrick, that grounding came from two pillars: faith and family.

I had the privilege of sharing a few thoughts for Jim's first book, *Beyond Theories and Degrees: The Alley Smarts of School Leadership*. That work demonstrated his deep understanding of leadership and how it's as much about the heart as it is about the head. This new memoir takes us even further—into the deep-seated values and closely-held convictions that sustain leaders over decades of service.

What strikes me about Jim's story is its honesty, authenticity, and true genuine nature. He doesn't romanticize leadership, nor does he shy away from the struggles and doubts that come with making high-stakes decisions affecting children, parents, families, and communities. Instead, he offers us a window into the real world of a superintendent and principal who carried the weight of responsibility—and did so, guided by a faith that was both personal and practical.

From his formative years in the Catholic tradition, to his experiences leading schools during times of economic stress, policy shifts, and cultural change, Jim illustrates a truth we too often overlook, that leadership is a human endeavor. It requires competence, yes—but also courage and compassion. And as Jim shows us, those qualities often flow from the deepest parts of who we are.

What I appreciate about Jim's book is how it blends memoir with mentorship. Readers can soak in the vivid stories—growing up in Lombard, Illinois; navigating the challenges of leading a school district; celebrating victories and surviving setbacks. But they will also find thoughtful, practical wisdom. At the end of each chapter, Jim reflects on lessons learned, offering insights that will resonate whether you are an aspiring leader, a veteran superintendent, or simply someone who cares deeply about the future of our schools.

Faith, in Jim's telling, is not about preaching or proselytizing. It's about hope. It's about finding strength when resources are scarce, clarity when decisions are complex, and grace when criticism is harsh. In an era when many leaders feel isolated and overwhelmed, this book serves as an important reminder that none of us leads alone.

I am honored to introduce *The Intersection of Faith and School Leadership*. It is more than a memoir—it is a testament to resilience, integrity, and the enduring power of belief. May it inspire you, as it inspired me, to lead with your heart as well as your head—and to never lose sight of what truly matters.

David R. Schuler, Ph.D.
Executive Director
AASA, The School Superintendents Association

Preface

One of my favorite songs, performed by Frank Sinatra is entitled *IT WAS A VERY GOOD YEAR*. There are four versus that beautifully chronicle a man's life journey and his reflections from teenage years through old age. As I have begun this project I can really relate to the fourth verse in reflecting upon my life:

> *"But now the days are short*
> *I'm in the autumn of the year*
> *And now I think of my life as vintage wine*
> *From fine old kegs*
> *From the brims to the dregs*
> *It poured sweet and clear*
> *It was a very good year!"*

This book has been a work in progress for many years. As I write these words, I, too, feel I am in the autumn of my life. At seventy-two years of age, I feel some pressure that I am racing against the clock to share my thoughts and reflections from boyhood to now, on what has truly been a blessed life.

So, what is it that would make me think that I might be able to write a book that others might find an interesting read? What would I have to offer that might give people a little enjoyment and maybe kick start others into reflecting upon their own lives? Well, I am presumptuous, or maybe bold enough to think there are people who might find my journey has some commonality with theirs, or some differences, that might prompt them to reflect upon their own lives and where they might be at present.

For me, everything starts with family. I was blessed to grow up in a loving family, as you will discover in the pages to follow. The strong under-pinning of being raised in a Catholic home has never abandoned me. I can't remember the last time I said a rosary, however, we grew up as a young family praying it often. While attending Sunday mass is something I have always done, it was not until adulthood and my most trying times that I realized how entrenched my faith was. My career and Catholicism have often intersected. At times, prayer was my last resort, and the good Lord almost always came through for me. And if I didn't get what I wanted, there was usually a good reason, maybe something even better down the road.

As a former superintendent, in a stressful time in my life in 2011, I prayed hard for God's intercession in helping my district pass a referendum. We won by four votes with five-thousand cast! God was looking down on me that day! The cut list I had in my drawer, had the referendum failed, never had to see the light of day. Do I believe in the power of prayer—You better believe it!

In this book, I list many mentors who helped me along the way. Hopefully this sparks you the reader to remember those great influencers in your life. Maybe it will motivate you to drop them a note, send them an email, or text, or even pick up the phone, thanking them for being a difference maker in your life. If they are no longer with us, remember them fondly from time to time in your meditation or prayers.

Another theme in this book is that both triumph and adversity are a part of our lives. Faith helps us get through the tough times and allows you to enjoy the great times, especially those special people who come into our lives. At the end of each chapter, I share the lessons I learned along the way, maybe they will resonate with you as well.

My son-in-law, BJ Reid has a saying; after talking with him, he often reminds me to "Keep the Faith!" And that is a good way to launch you into this book, along with wishing you all of God's Blessings.

James E. Fitzpatrick

The Intersection of Faith and School Leadership: The Memoirs of a School Administrator

Introduction

As I begin this book, there are two early childhood memories entrenched in my mind that to this day, I remember vividly in understanding that my upbringing as a Catholic in the Chicago suburb of Lombard, would have an everlasting impact on my life.

The Chicago White Sox had not won a pennant since the 1919 Black Sox scandal. Throughout the fifties, the White Sox had some great teams, led by Billy Pierce, Nellie Fox, Luis Aparicio, and Sherman Lollar. However, they never had the power or overall talent to overtake the powerful Yankees with Mickey Mantle, Yogi Berra, and Whitey Ford.

My father, James Raymond Fitzpatrick, was a south-sider and a passionate White Sox fan. In 1959, it was the Cleveland Indians, not the Yankees, who were battling the White Sox for the pennant. On the night of September 22nd, the Sox had the chance to clinch their first pennant in forty years! They had the game seemingly in hand until the ninth inning, when the Sox ace Early Wynn, who had held the Indians in check, got into trouble loading the bases. Manager Al Lopez then called upon reliever Gerry Staley. It was then that my dad made my two sisters and me, along with my mom, kneel down and say a Hail Mary, as the dangerous Vic Power came to the plate. God answered our prayers! In one pitch, Staley got Power to hit a ground ball that shortstop Luis Aparicio fielded, stepping on second and then firing to first for a game ending double play! At long last, the White Sox were the American League Champions!

The game was barely over ten minutes, and neighbor pals of my dad, also Sox fans, were pounding on the door, screaming for my dad to join them to greet the pennant winning White Sox at MIDWAY Airport on their arrival back from Cleveland. I remember my mom smiling and saying; "Go!" Well, what I learned years later, is that they made a few stops on the way, and were feeling no pain by the time they got to Midway. At least the guy who drove was able to find his way back home! My dad like many of his generation, worked really hard to support our family. He also played hard and loved to party! The Sox clinching the 1959 pennant was one of those nights!

The air-raid sirens in Chicago went off! Mayor Richard J. Daley and Fire Commissioner Robert Quinn, both White Sox fans, took a lot of heat for alarming Chicago residents who, during the Cold War, thought the Russians were invading. However, Chicagoans quickly got over it once they realized their beloved Sox would be facing the Dodgers in the World Series.

My second recollection of my early Catholicism came when John Kennedy was elected president. I remember my parents' placing buttons on our jackets that we wore to school stating; "If I were 21, I would vote for KENNEDY." All the kids on the bus on the way to Sacred Heart School in Lombard, Illinois, had similar buttons. We would sing: *"Kennedy is going to the White House, waiting to be elected, Nixon is in the garbage can waiting to be collected."* There was such excitement that for the first time ever, a Catholic might be elected to the White House!

On Election Night, my parents let us stay up later than usual as the returns came in. By ten o'clock, we were sent to bed not knowing who won. I will never forget the look on my Dad's face when we woke up the next morning to get ready for school. I asked my Dad – who won? I remember the cautious smile, and his words; "They think Jack's got it."

Well, at 7:15 AM, just before we left the house for the bus stop, NBC had declared Kennedy the winner by a scant 120,000 votes out of over sixty-eight million cast! My Dad made the three of us and my mother, once again, say a Hail Mary in thanksgiving for the election outcome. Our bus ride to school was just crazy. All the kids on our block were jumping for joy, feeding off our parents. I remember the bus driver yelling at all of us to sit down and be quiet. I think he was for Nixon!

As I reflect upon the above, now in my seventies, it seems amazing to me that such deep foundational roots can take hold at such an early age. As you turn the pages of this book the Faith foundation always seemed to surface in every stage of my life, whether I realized it or not.

I hope you enjoy this book as I take you through a life that has been enriching for me in so many ways. If it moves you as the reader to laughter, maybe a couple of tears, but mostly joy for a life filled with many blessings, then this book will have served its purpose. It's also my wish that this book will serve as a reflective tool for you to think back with deep appreciation for the loved ones, mentors, and people who decided to invest in you, in helping you maximize your personal potential, along with instilling in you a desire to pay it forward in helping others achieve their dreams.

Chapter 1

The Early Years: Mom and Dad

I remember when we were a family of three children before my brother Tony's arrival in November of 1958. Maryann, the oldest, and Kathryn (who we call KK for Kathryn Kennedy) was the youngest, with me in the middle as the second oldest. Life seemed simple in those days. Many World War II veterans used the GI Bill for low interest loans to purchase their first homes. After being apartment dwellers, my parents, like many young Chicago families, moved out to the suburbs.

Mom with me, KK, Tony, and Maryann

My Mom referred to our new digs as the farm fields of Lombard, as we settled into the sub-division of Highland Hills! Our modest one-level ranch style home had three small bedrooms, a small living room, a combined kitchen-dining room, and one bathroom, with an attached garage, that would later be converted into a family room/bedroom combination as our family continued to grow. After Tony was born in 1958, four more siblings would follow in the next seven years Kevin, Therese Maria, Jean Marie, and Annemarie! We were the typical good Irish Catholic family in the neighborhood.

Early family picture in 1958–Kathryn (KK), Dad, Tony (baby), Maryann, and me

Our block was filled with kids, so it was very easy to make friends. There were no busy streets or intersections. In the summer, kids swarmed the streets and the spacious backyards. There were always games to play, whiffle ball, softball, kickball, drive-way basketball and hockey, football, and kick the can, a favorite game we played on summer nights after dinner where we would hide behind houses, bushes, and trees hoping to rush to the street to "kick the can" before being seen and declared OUT! The only thing that could break up a game was the Good Humor Ice Cream truck coming down your block. Everyone raced back to their houses to squeeze a nickel or dime out of their parents for a popsicle.

I remember mothers would gather and have conversations and mid-morning breaks. At the time, they were all in their mid to upper twenties. This was their therapy in those days. These returning GI fathers and mothers still struggled to make ends meet with their growing families. I remember Dad's getting together in a garage at night listening to a Sox or Cub game while having a couple of beers. Even the parish priests would stop by once in a while and tip one with the dads.

Some of the best education came from the bus stops, where we waited to be transported to Sacred Heart School. This is where I learned some of my first dirty words. The bus ride had first graders all the way up to eighth graders all mixed in! This was also where you met kids who lived on the other blocks nestled in the Highland Hills sub-division. Eventually, we meandered to the other blocks in the neighborhood, meeting a growing number of friends. I recall thinking how huge 7th and 8th graders looked and you better not smart off to them! Meeting them again in adulthood made you lose some of that trepidation, but not all! We had some pretty rough guys in our neighborhood.

Sacred Heart was bursting at the seams! So was St. Pius X, another Catholic elementary school in Lombard. I remember in first grade asking the nun how many treats I should bring for my birthday. She told me "61"! Wow, as I look back as retired principal, I always thought anything more than twenty-five pupils was getting too big! After fourth grade, a new Catholic Parish and School, Christ the King, opened to serve our neighborhood. My Mom and Dad became very active parishioners.

My parents, Jim and Annamae Fitzpatrick somehow raised eight of us! Now, as I look back, and as the father of two adult children, (and now a grandpa of two boys) I marvel at how they did it! It sometimes pains me to think of all the nicer things they could have had in life. They were totally invested in us, making sure that all eight of us had not necessarily everything we wanted, but definitely what we really needed to succeed!

My Dad, as mentioned, was a south-sider who graduated from St. Leo High School in May of 1943. He had worked in a funeral home during his high school years to help his mother, a widow with six children. Shortly after high school graduation, he enlisted in the Navy and soon after found himself in the Pacific theater during World War II. He served as a pharmacist's mate on the USS Noble, a transport ship.

Dad in the Navy during World War 2

My Dad rarely wanted to talk about the war, but one thing I really remember is that he hated guns and would not even allow for toy guns to be brought in the house. He was also very tense around the fourth of July and had no tolerance for neighbors popping off firecrackers at night. I was never able to verify it, but I think I heard that the transport ship he was on returned some of the marines who were involved in the Batoon Death March in the Philippines. While he had a great love and passion for our country and was proud to have served in the Navy, his hatred for war was always evident. There was a popular TV series in the sixties entitled *Combat*. All the neighborhood kids would talk about it on bus rides to school. My Dad would never allow us to watch it.

After the Navy, he enrolled in Worsham College of Mortuary Science, where he earned his Funeral Director License. He became a trade embalmer while also directing funerals, and selling caskets. Later, and for the rest of his career he sold burial vaults, mostly for the Wilbert Burial Vault Company. I remember as a young kid, how he would work night and day for various funeral homes in the western suburbs.

My mother was raised on the West side graduating from St Catherine of Sienna High School in Oak Park. She was a great writer and had a scholarship to Northwestern. However, even with the scholarship offer, times were tough. Instead of remaining at Northwestern, she dropped out after a semester and worked at Walgreens, also volunteering at Hines Hospital VA for veterans. My Mom helped her mother, who was widowed young, and her grandmother as they tried to make ends meet in the forties.

Picture of Mom, and her favorite Maya Angelou quote

My Dad, and Mom, came to some sort of understanding that with a growing family, eventually eight kids, someone always had to be home. However, times got tough as I recall beginning in my sixth-grade year. I do remember vividly the utilities company shutting off our electricity for a day before my Dad could somehow scrape up enough money to pay the bill. I remember us having candles lit that night. My Mom made the most of it, there we were with our first experience as kids with a candlelight dinner. I almost remember us feeling somewhat upset when the power was eventually turned back on. I can't say for sure, but I think our grandmother Mae McGuire (Mamie) came through with the money needed to pay off the utilities bill.

Even in challenging times, we always had enough to eat, clean clothes, and a roof over our head. Sunday dinners at 1:00 PM, were especially memorable. We always had a great meal with my grandma, great grandma, and Uncle Gene joining us. My Mom was a fabulous cook. My favorite was fried chicken, but we had ham, pork roasts, and roast beef as well with potatoes and great salads. Another thing I remember is that some of our friends were also welcomed at times. Tim Smith and Frank Harrison two of my buddies often ate with us over the years. Same was true for my siblings and their friends. We often had invited guests for a Sunday or Holiday dinner.

My father had a heart attack in the spring of my sixth-grade year. Looking back this was probably the rock bottom point in our family history. At this point we were a family of seven kids and making ends meet had to be stressful. My Dad was working night and day, often not eating healthy when he could not be home, and he put on a lot of weight. His blood pressure was sky high when he had to be rushed to the hospital the night of the heart attack. My mother was a nervous wreck, even in her greatest moment of angst, she told my Dad, *"look pal with all these kids you are not going to take the cowards way out; you are the provider, and you need to get well."* I think Dad took her little pep talk to heart. Back in those days' heart attack patients remained in the hospital for about three weeks before being discharged. My Dad's hospital room was on the first floor of the hospital, my Mom thought maybe Maryann, KK, and me, the three oldest could wave to him through the window. Dad would have none of it, and let my Mom know he did not want his kids to see him in this condition. I remember my Mom crying, she was at her wit's end. It's only now as I record these memories, that I finally understand the stress my Mom and Dad had been under in supporting our family.

My Mom found a job at Pepperidge Farms where she worked a graveyard shift from nine o'clock PM to five o'clock AM. My Dad hated that she had to work. He was driven to be the provider for our family! And he was! However, he finally needed some help, and Mom came through. She was very sensitive to my Dad's indignant feelings of unhappiness that his wife had to work. Initially he resisted the idea, only giving in under the condition that once he was back on his feet, he wanted her to quit! In working the graveyard shift, Mom thought she could keep it a secret from the neighbors, but eventually friends in the neighborhood knew about it.

My Dad eventually did get back on his feet after his heart attack. He took a new job at Wilbert Vault Company in Forest Park, Illinois. He was an amazing salesman! Every funeral director in Illinois knew him. In fact, he once was elected President of the Illinois Funeral Directors Association. The three oldest (Maryann, KK, and myself) every morning would look at the death notices in the early editions of the Chicago Tribune and Sun Times, along with my Dad at the breakfast table to see what funeral home accounts were handling funeral arrangements, where surely a burial vault would need to be ordered.

One of the demands of my Dad's new job at Wilbert Vault was that he often had to take clients (funeral directors) out golfing at the company's country-club and then out to dinner. He was out very late at night and even into the early mornings on many of these occasions. His boss demanded that he "stay out and show these guys a good time, it would be good for business," and it was!

However, it was not good on the home front. My Mom working the night shift at Pepperidge Farms, would call my oldest sister Maryann to have her check on all the babies. At that time there were three under five-years of age. I would be very remiss if I were not to acknowledge the great efforts of Maryann who in many ways served like a "second mom" during those years. She was a huge help to my mother as was KK the second oldest daughter who along with Maryann incurred a lot of responsibilities at a pretty young age. I love all my siblings but it's only now that I have really come to understand just how Maryann and KK helped keep our family together and functioning as my Mom and Dad struggled during these difficult couple of years.

Dad could "work a room" like nobody else. Whether at work, a party, or a gathering, nobody could tell a joke like he could. His boss saw this in him and really liked the idea of having Dad ingratiate clients whether it was in calling on them as customers or wining and dining them. I swear he could have been a comedian with his comments and gestures. I remember even as a young kid how people seemed to flock to him when he would be relating a story or sharing a joke. He would have people in stiches! To this day all eight of us often share his quips and funny comments we remember from our childhood, including when he was really ticked off at us! Even in anger, he had some lines that are unforgettable. One example if you were not getting your way on something was his response; "well too bad, the people in hell want ice water."

Dad was also a tough disciplinarian. He insisted on manners. We responded to our parents as "yes sir, and yes ma'am." To his credit neighbors and adults often shared that the "Fitzpatrick kids are the politest kids you will ever meet." Back then, I never realized how this training and grounding would serve all eight of us so well in our adult lives.

In our house, you better be on time for dinner, and you better make darn sure you completed a chore Dad expected of you. I sometimes wish in those days Dad would have known about TIME OUTS when kids acted up. Of course, whether he would have used them is another story! If you ticked him off or were disrespectful, you could expect a backhand across the mouth or a painful yank of your hair (maybe that is why I am bald now)! He was gentler with my sisters but still firm with them on rules. The three of us boys did get the belt when we had it coming. I think my brother Tony (who is the most like my Dad), holds the record!

Dad was also a stickler on curfew. If you were a minute late by his watch you were grounded for the next weekend. We were not allowed to go out on school nights. After dishes, we did our homework at the kitchen table. I thought by the time I was twenty and home from college for the summer, he might give me a pass on the curfews he still imposed on the five youngest kids. No such luck! I remember one Friday night about 8 PM, I said "I am going out to see some friends. He said okay, be in by eleven! I said; "eleven, you gotta be kidding me, cripes I am going to be a junior in college, eighth graders get to stay out until eleven!" Taking the ever-present cigar out of his mouth he lowered the newspaper he was reading and said, "okay make it ten-thirty!" I left the house in a huff, thinking if I continued to argue, he would make it nine o'clock!

Dad and his ever-present cigar at a sister's wedding

Mom was the one if you wanted something really bad, you went to her first. She could say no, but not as readily as Dad. One of the things every one of our eight kids figured out, is that my Dad could never refuse my Mom. But Mom had an abundance of wisdom in discerning what was reasonable to get Dad to approve or change his mind about when we wanted her to intercede for us.

Mom also could pick up very quickly if something was really bothering us or if for some reason we were seemingly sad or depressed. Dad occasionally noticed such times, but not as astutely as Mom. She was amazing in how she could become so involved in each or our lives and give us advice and ideas that were so spot on! Even well into my career as I became a superintendent of schools in Wisconsin, she somehow could really sense what I might be going through during difficult times. Her suggestions even in not being a school person often made a lot of sense!

Once the youngest five of the Fitzpatrick children were in high school, college, or off to work, Mom decided she wanted to work outside the home, but not full time. She found work at Kammes Reality in nearby Wheaton, Illinois. Her boss loved her and it was not long before she was making a big impact at this Reality Office! Mr. Kammes begged her to work full-time but she begged off for family reasons, still feeling the need to be home. Her income certainly helped with college tuition and other things that came up.

I now often wonder "what if my Mom would have finished at Northwestern?" I honestly believe that her selfless sacrifice for our family and always being there for us, might have been the greatest act of love I have ever witnessed. That said, I also believe that while we wait for many women to break glass ceilings in our society, Mom could have shattered it to pieces had she gone on to get her degree and pursued a career. Her creativity, intuitiveness, and imagination were only exceeded by her love for us!

Mom had so much wisdom! As an example, Maryann, the oldest, once shared with my Mom that the younger kids seemed to have things easier. Mom's response was "that is true, we can afford more material things for them now, but you oldest three had our youth!" What a great response! On another occasion, I complained to my Mom that Dad was really too hard on us. Her response: "If it was not for him, you kids would have run all over me. And if it wasn't for me he would have killed every one of you!" Her assessment here was probably not far from the truth!

I would be very remiss if I were not to mention another important role model in my life, Uncle Gene McGuire. He was my mother's only sibling. He worked for L.E. Meyers (Electrical contractors) of Chicago for most of his adult life. Like my Dad he was a veteran. He served in the Army, stationed in Europe. While our family is deeply rooted in the Catholic Faith, which included two cousins who entered the priesthood, and two nuns in the Mercy order, Uncle Gene was the most fervent and faithful Catholic I have ever met.

Something I figured out later in life was that from second to eighth grade, my parents often shipped me off to Uncle Gene's and Grandma Mamie's on weekends. They lived in a small apartment on Austin Boulevard in Oak Park, barely outside the Chicago city-limits. I think this was done to relieve the household in Lombard that was bursting at the seams with all of our kids.

On those weekends, Uncle Gene would take me to mass. He went every day of the week, often serving mass or lectoring. Afterward, we would usually go to breakfast and then to a Cub or White Sox game, but mostly Cubs. Uncle Gene had a grandstand pass at Wrigley, and in those days twenty-two thousand seats went on sale the day of the game. It was first come first serve for the grandstand seats, so I literally nagged Uncle Gene to get there early so we could watch batting practice! I loved baseball and the Chicago teams. He would also play catch with me in the alley, or take me to Columbus Park where he could hit fly balls to me.

When I signed up to be an altar boy at Christ the King parish in the summer before 5th grade, Uncle Gene was tasked with teaching me the Latin mass server responses. He was relentless in his kind way of making sure no altar server would know his Latin better than me.

About a year later, following Vatican 2 and the Church's effort to modernize the mass in native languages, my Latin skills were no longer necessary; now I had to learn the responses in English, some more studying with Uncle Gene! To this day, I can still recite the Confiteor and the *prayers at the Foot of the Altar* in Latin. Uncle Gene was the kind of teacher who made sure you retained what he taught you!

It was not until later that I learned that Uncle Gene had gone to the seminary in Cape Girardeau, Missouri, to become a priest. He was so devout, yet he came to the conclusion that he was not worthy enough to become a priest. That to me is one of the mysteries of my life. I never met a holier man. When the Cubs won the World Series in 2016, I am positive up in Heaven, he had something to do with the miracle in Cleveland on November 2, 2016.

As I conclude this chapter, I am ashamed to acknowledge that I had to become a high school principal to realize just how blessed and fortunate I was to have such loving and caring parents. As a school man, I have worked with so many youths, who never had the love, nurturing and foundational underpinning of a good home.

From Dad, I learned to always be a stand-up guy. Be honest, work hard, and don't complain. He was also an optimist, a glass half-full guy. His humor was contagious. I have some of those trait's thanks to him! From my Mom I learned the importance of kindness, being a good listener, and reaching out to people who have fallen on tough times. As I type these words, I remember when a family in the neighborhood was going through a tough time, she would send me over to their home with a fresh loaf of homemade bread, or sometimes oatmeal cookies and brownies. Our family didn't have much, but from my Mom I learned whatever you do have, be willing to share. The most meaningful gestures and gifts one can extend to another come from the heart more than the wallet, and the recipients of that kindness never forget!

In closing Mom and Dad's marriage was by no means perfect, they fought a lot, usually about money and how to make ends meet. Recently, I listened to a priest who defined the perfect marriage as ***"an imperfect husband and an imperfect wife who absolutely refuse to give up on one another! That's a perfect marriage!*** That was my Mom and Dad, and that is what I believe is the underpinning of my own marriage to my wife Therese, as we just celebrated our forty-eighth anniversary.

Summary thoughts and takeaways from this chapter!

- Faith is powerful, it sometimes takes years before you realize how entrenched your faith is as a part of your moral fiber!
- Great parents are often under-appreciated until you become a parent yourself!
- Work hard, have a sense of humor, and care about people - this will always serve you well.
- Have a good outlook, the glass is always half full, even in the worst of circumstances. Instead of worrying about challenges, look more for opportunities.
- No act of kindness is ever too small. A loaf of homemade bread can bring someone the comfort they need.
- It's a marvelous experience to witness a marriage full of challenges where the couple never falls out of love for one

another. That was my parents and the underpinning of my marriage to my wife Therese the past forty-eight years.

Today, with horrific mass shootings, COVID, political divisiveness, and devastating fires and floods, global warming, unrest in the Middle East and in Ukraine, it seems we are always facing a crisis. Looking back to my childhood and adolescent years, it just seemed to be an easier time to grow up. In upcoming chapters, I attempt to sequentially highlight through my life journey just how important relationships and mentors are in our lives. They help us navigate through the tough times, along with helping us become our best selves. And for me it all started with family and faith!

Chapter 2

Boyhood Memories!

By the time I hit fifth grade, playing sports was just about the only thing I cared about. In school, I dreaded report card day, but usually managed to do just enough to keep my parents from grounding me. In the summer, we played whiffle ball, softball, and baseball. In the fall, we played football and driveway basketball. When winter came, we played basketball whenever we could sneak into a gym or play on a shoveled off driveway, or street hockey, and with the last snow and the promise of spring, we began the cycle all over again.

One of my favorite memories was being in Little League. I played two years when I was 11 and 12. For some reason, Dad and Mom thought I should wait until then instead of starting at nine. Besides I was playing with neighborhood kids every day! Kids back then organized their own games. Nowadays, it seems to me parents get too over involved in organizing play and recreation for their kids. Sports camps, expensive travel teams, clubs, AAU-- parents control everything and I wonder if sports burnout is a reason you rarely see a three-sport student-athlete in high school anymore.

My Little League team was the Yankees. Well as it turned out, the Yankees, who were in last place the year before, had some nice returning players that were still on the team. One player was Mike Dingman (pseudonym), who lived across the street from us. He was head and shoulders above the best player in the league. He never lost a game he pitched and he threw very hard and had an unbelievable curve ball for a twelve-year old. He also was a great hitter! I can't remember him ever making an out! He was also fast, and if he didn't hit one over the fence, he could beat out any grounder he hit.

My Yankee coach Bill Neuman, was the perfect little league coach. Upon reflection of all the coaches I had as a high school and collegiate athlete, he ranks among the best I ever had.

I remember one of the first things Coach Neuman did before the first game was to talk to the parents in the bleachers behind our bench. I can still hear his voice: *"Rule number one: I don't want to ever hear any parent yelling or criticizing this team, our opponent, or the umpires. These kids are going to learn how to be baseball players, and while we are at it they are going to learn sportsmanship! I will do the coaching and teach them the fundamentals, so I don't need your advice or input unless I ask you for it. Rule number two: After every game, win or lose I expect the kids to be treated to a bag of popcorn and a soda. And if I have to buy it after every game, I will do it!"* He never had to buy. The parents all stepped up and organized a list for every game, with parents taking turns.

Turning twelve, and at the risk of being a bit immodest, I was a pretty good little catcher and I made the All-Star team. We won our first all-star game. We all thought we were on our way to the Williamsport World Series Championship. I remember Bob Blackburn, an older kid in the neighborhood bringing us back to reality; "You guys aren't that good." He was right. The next night we lost to a really good team from Maywood, Illinois!

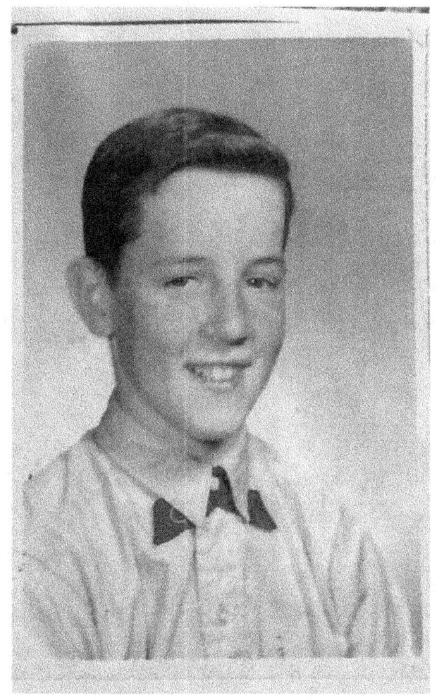

Sixth grade picture at Christ the King school

It's funny the things you remember. My sixth-grade little league year was the same year my Dad had his heart attack, so he missed almost all of my games. It was not until late in the season that he was out of the hospital and could attend a game. It was the fourth inning of the title game, where whoever won would be the League champion. Our team was down 2-1. The bases were loaded with two outs when I came to the plate. The first two pitches, I swung hard and missed. I was pressing, my Dad was there, and I wanted so bad for him to see how well I had been playing. It was then that Coach Bill Neuman called a time out and beckoned me over to the third base coaching box where he stood. He says to me; *"Jimmy, I just heard that your dad had a heart attack.* I replied, "yes, he just got out of the hospital last week." I can still see Neuman's blue eyes and he said to me; *"get back in the box and forget that your dad is even here."* On the next pitch, I hit a double off the center field fence, clearing the bases and breaking the game wide open.

I can still remember my Dad's voice yelling "nice hit Ace" (my nickname), and coach Neuman looking at me from the third base coaching box with those piercing blue eyes and making a fist and nodding his approval without saying a word. Oh, did that feel good! Bill Neuman was one of those youth coaches truly in it for the right reasons. An early mentor, not just a coach, but an unforgettable influence.

A lot of adults my age like to share their Catholic School experiences. Why not? For the most part, they are joyous and fun memories. Usually, you can detect a little embellishment when the topic of the nuns comes up.

One such nun was Sister Lucille (pseudonym) in 5th grade. She could be very sweet one minute and scare the living hell out of you the next. I think most Catholic kids with good penmanship would have to credit the good sisters for their fastidious efforts in getting children to write neatly. I am a living example of where the nuns failed in this endeavor.

One day, we all had to bring our spelling books up to Sister Lucille. We did this row by row. My particular row had some guys with terrible penmanship, but none as bad as mine. It did not help that I was the fifth and last guy in the row, and Sister Lucille was already warmed up, very angry, and screaming! When it was my turn to set my speller in front of her, she went into hysterics. She screamed, *"Fitzpatrick, look at this —just look at it!"* She then took her pen and ripped the page right out of the spelling book, then she gave me a good stab with the pen right in the stomach, it really smarted! I was darn near on the brink of tears just out of fright. To this day classmates of mine from Christ the King remembered that day more than 60 years ago! It seems funny now, but it's a wonder I didn't wet my pants or something even worse!

About a month later the Mother Superior was coming by for her annual inspection, and Sister Lucille a couple days before her visit told me to stay after school. So, I did, and she said; *"bring me your speller, Jimmy."* Well in her beautiful handwriting, she inserted a piece of paper that listed all of the spelling words on the page she had ripped out of my speller with her pen. After she was done, I put it back on the shelf. I am quite sure Mother Superior thought this careless student wrecked the page, and good Sister Lucille took the time to replace it.

A strategy the nuns would employ at times was getting your parents' signature on a half-hearted assignment that you turned in. The hope was that your parents would really get after you-which they did, and that would be the end of sub-par efforts. Right after President Kennedy was assassinated, we were assigned to write either a one-page composition or a poem about President Kennedy. Again, this was in fifth grade with Sister Lucille. I took the liberty of paraphrasing the poem *Trees* by Joyce Kilmer. So, in the first short stanza, I wrote, *I think that I shall never know a man who loved his country so!* I went on to stretch this out to four short stanzas that rhymed pretty well!

Well, Sister Lucille thought it was terrible! Admittedly, my penmanship was not good, and I misspelled some words. I was sweating bullets before I showed it to my father, fearing a possible grounding, but had a pleasant surprise! He wrote: *"penmanship-atrocious, spelling-even worse, but content EXCELLENT!"* I had a pretty good smirk on my face when I turned this in to Sister Lucille, by gosh, my Dad had my back!

Knowing what I know now having been a principal or superintendent most of my career, there were some real abuses back in those days. We had some special education students in our classes who had legitimate learning disabilities and they were verbally abused by Sister Lucille as lazy and non-compliant. That was not good. I often wonder what became of a couple of these young classmates back in fifth grade.

I do know my sister Kathryn (KK), who has the most analytical, engineering, and problem-solving mind in our family, was a victim of nun cruelty. After high school and college, she would hold high level jobs with Illinois Bell and later Comcast Cable Corporation! KK entered kindergarten at age 4 with an October birthday. So, she was very young in her grade level. For some reason, Sister Adrian (pseudonym), would just be mean and say nasty things to her.

Most of the Catholic parents I knew growing up had blind faith in the nuns and priests. In other words, if you did something wrong at school you could be assured there would be consequences at home, if your mom and Dad found out about it. My parents were generally of this mindset, however after fourth grade, they had enough of Sister Adrian. They pulled KK out and enrolled her in the nearby public school, where she flourished. After eighth grade, she followed me to Montini Catholic High School, where she was a year behind me. My parents never knew about all of my issues with Sister Lucille, but if they had, I might have followed KK to the Lombard public schools.

In sixth grade, I had a wonderful teacher named Sister Carol (pseudonym). This was a really hard year for our family, especially toward the end of the school year when my Dad had his heart attack in April. Before that, there were signs that Mom and Dad were really struggling to make ends meet. This was the same year that a guy from the utilities company came over and shut off our electricity in late

November. My mom just had her seventh baby the previous April. Number eight (Annmarie, the baby of the family) would soon be on the way.

The night of my Dad's heart attack, I remember coming home from Little League practice and Mr. Pawley, a close friend and neighbor of our family, was there to tell me that my Dad had to be ambulanced to the hospital. Later, we would learn that he had a heart attack. The next morning after Mass and just before class was to begin, Sister Carol came up to me, put her arms around me, and gave me a hug, telling me "your dad will pull through, he is a strong man." She made it her business to know what was going on in the Christ the King neighborhoods.

About two weeks after my Dad's heart attack, there was a field trip to St. Charles Borromeo Seminary for the boys. We were often taught about listening for a calling to the religious life. We were told to dress up in our Sunday best. The hope was that there might be a couple of future seminarians among us, and indeed there were! My best friend, Tim Smith, attended the seminary for three years. I really thought at one point he might go all the way to ordination. I think girls and baseball got in the way. He became a star pitcher in high school our senior year, and he dated a gorgeous girl.

Just as we were getting lined up to get on the bus for the seminary, Sister Renee pseudonym), came up to me. I had high-top gym shoes on. My feet were growing fast, and my mom was getting me shoes at this discount store about every two months for like $2.99. I did have a sport coat on that was a little short in the sleeves, but passable, and some school uniform pants that were nicely pressed by my mom before I left the house.

Well, Sister Renee knew about the messaging of wearing your Sunday best. She came up to me and stepped on my shoes, and asked, "where are your dress shoes?" In a smart-ass tone, in front of all my peers, I told her *"I didn't feel like wearing any dress shoes today, and too bad if you don't like it."* My parents being from the greatest generation and Irish, taught us to never cry the poor mouth. I was really embarrassed, and I surprised myself with the words that came out of my mouth, I had always to that point been a pretty respectful kid!

Well, just in the nick of time, Sister Carol appeared on the scene. She asked Sister Renee to come into the office. I remember seeing through the blinds of the office Sister Carol, all five foot one of her on her tip toes, pointing her finger into Sister Renee's face. Undoubtedly giving her the word about the struggles the Fitzpatrick family were going through.

Sister Carol then came out before we got on the bus and pulled me aside. She straightened my lapel collar out, and said, *"Jimmy, get on that bus and have a good day!"* And then she gave me that million-dollar hug! I thought the tears were going to rush from my eyelids like Niagara Falls! I had all I could do in holding them back, but somehow I did! I got on the bus and had a fun day with my classmates!

When I reflect on this experience, I realize that within a matter of 5 minutes or less, I had one of the most horrible experiences of my life, followed by one of the greatest acts of kindness ever shown to me. Sister Carol, I will always cherish her moment of intercession! That was another experience that made me feel blessed that good people do look out for you!

Later in my life, as I pursued positions of school leadership, the influence of Sister Carol never abandoned me. Her kindness, empathy, and compassion are the same traits I have seen in the greatest leaders I have observed and tried to emulate in my practice. I hope one day, maybe in Heaven (if I get there) I can meet her again and tell her just how grateful I was that day of the seminary field trip.

Well, how could seventh grade be better after having Sister Carol for sixth grade? It was pretty uneventful. Sports, far more than academics, remained my main focus. One memory that stands out was making the eighth-grade basketball team when I was in seventh grade. Fifteen guys made the team, but only five were seventh graders. I did not get much action, but I was learning how to play and toward the end of the season, Mr. Budi our coach was giving me more minutes.

Another favorite activity was getting out of class to serve funeral masses. They were usually scheduled at about ten o'clock in the morning. I became an expert at signing up to serve funeral masses for Father Pryer (pseudonym), just so I could get out of math class. Another incentive was that the funeral directors might slip us a couple of bucks!

Father Pryer was a pretty cool guy. At the funerals, we would try to see who could put the most incense in and make it look like the church was going up in smoke. However, Father always warned us that one small charcoal was enough. I put three in one time and he was squinting so hard, that even he had to chuckle on how smoky we got it. It was so thick you could not see the casket and the first row of pews from the altar. Pretty soon you heard a lot of coughing! After that funeral, Father put me off the serving detail for the next month, but he did tell me that was the best SMOKE he had ever seen!

Somehow, we all got promoted to eighth grade. Once again, we had Sister Lucille, who was also the principal of the school. Looking back, that is sort of a head scratcher! We were bolder and not quite as afraid of her as we were in fifth grade. We could predict when the hysterics would be coming. She was often out of the classroom attending to administrative matters. She might be out of the room for an hour at a time, and maybe a room mother or secretary would peek in as we were assigned work sheets to work on independently.

I could hardly wait for basketball to begin in November. I spent a lot of time practicing my shooting and dribbling. Every chance I got I would get into driveway pickup games in our neighborhood, often playing against older guys, which helped me get better. I was a five-feet four and playing guard. We didn't win many games, but after Christmas we started to gel. We ended the season with a losing record however we improved quite a bit from the beginning of the season to the end. Mr. Budi, our coach who could drive us pretty hard, was happy with the progress we had made. I had a good season leading the team in scoring. I was voted by my team-mates to be on the All-Star team.

One of the highlights of our eighth-grade year was putting on the play *OUR TOWN*, by Thornton Wilder. Looking back that was a pretty ambitious undertaking for seventh and eighth grade kids. Mr. Jackson (pseudonym), the science teacher actually directed the play. I was Howie Newsome, the milk man. To this day, I still remember my lines as my cameo appearance depicted me on a horse and buggy (using a milk crate with me holding an imaginary harness), and delivering milk and cream to Mrs. Webb (Roberta Brink) and Mrs. Gibbs (Geri Burmeister). Both were real cuties! My buddy Tim Smith had a major lead as Dr. Gibbs. He did not mind one bit walking through the heliotropes in a scene with Geri! At our fifty-year high school reunion, I caught up with Roberta (Mrs. Webb) and got a laugh out of her when I recited the lines we had in the play.

By - eighth grade my pals and I were becoming more attracted to our female classmates. It's funny to think back now how we would get a message to a girl that we liked. In today's world there might be a text or social media way to convey such feelings. Back then, you might ask a girl to tell the girl you really liked to convey the message, and hopefully bring back good news that the feeling was mutual. I remember telling Susie Maloney, who sat next to me in class, that I really liked Mary Budi, the daughter of the basketball coach. I wondered if she would go to the church bazaar with me? Well, Susie didn't waste any time, and came back to me saying Mary was wondering if I would ever ask, because she saw me looking at her often in class. We did go to the Bazaar, played some games, ate some pizza, and had a fun time.

Now I was ready for the big time- the 8th grade cotillion, where eighth graders at Christ the King were invited to their first teen club dance shortly after graduation. I guess this was really my first official date with Mary. We agreed to meet up at the dance, not wanting our parents to know that we were sort of a thing. It was really a fun time, with a great band. Mary was the first girl I had ever held hands or slow danced with, and I must say, I was liking it. While we went to the same high school and remained friends, we never formally dated, but looking back I would have to say she was my first crush.

Following my 8th grade graduation and looking forward to enrolling at Montini High School the following Fall, my first job making money was at Glen Oak Country Club where I caddied. It was pretty good money for a fourteen-year-old, and I made enough to cover my tuition in my freshman and sophomore years. The caddy shack at Glen Oak was like the Master's Degree program for learning profanity and off-color expressions. I never became a good golfer myself, but I caddied for some good players, and I got good at knowing what clubs to suggest, and I knew all the distances to the greens, plus I could usually find an errant ball in the rough or weeds. Pretty soon, club members would request that the caddy master assign me for their round if I was available.

Christ the King Grade 6 class picture 1965, I am in third desk in second row from the right. My buddy Tim Smith first desk, in first row on the right

In looking back on my elementary years, there was a lot of formative training that I never really appreciated in shaping who I am. At Christ the King, the experience that most vividly stands out was in 5th grade when President Kennedy was assassinated. It remains truly one of the saddest days of my life. The first time I ever experienced grief. That whole weekend was surreal for a fifth grader to comprehend. Upon hearing the news of the shooting, we were in church five minutes later, saying the Rosary before getting the final word that the president had indeed died from the gun shots. At that point, the church just seemed to be the right place to be.

Later in life as a superintendent, we experienced the attack on the twin towers on September 11, 2001, with nearly three-thousand people losing their lives. We struggled as to how we would work with our students during this crisis, especially the younger elementary children. Every school now has emergency crisis plans to address the traumatic experiences that children and adolescents in our K-12 school districts have now been exposed to since the Columbine school shootings. In looking back, I think our little learning community at Christ the King was well served being in church, and saying the rosary on that fateful day November 22, 1963.

As I close this chapter and look back on my early Catholic school experiences, I really cherish them. Christ the King had quite an influence on me and who I am today. Even Sister Lucille whom in the previous pages I was a little tough on. Deep down, I really liked her. There were times she was very nice to me, and I often enjoyed pleasing her by cleaning chalk boards, and shoveling the walk between the convent and the school. Looking back, I think she had a lot on her plate, being a principal and a classroom teacher. I even wonder if at times she had nervous breakdowns. She had a saying; *"only good fish- swim upstream."* She repeated it often, and it has stuck with me my whole life, especially when times get tough. A good thing to remember as I moved on to high school.

Summary thoughts and takeaways from this chapter!

- Lead like Sister Carol, if you see something that is inherently wrong-address it and make it right.
- Never be afraid to stand up to mean people. Kind and compassionate leadership always attracts followership.
- It's nice to be an all-star, but we also need to be humble enough to accept cameo roles that contribute to the success of the group or organization. Being a good team-mate is honorable.
- Like Bill Neuman's advice "get back in the box"-be able to compartmentalize and focus when there is a task that needs concentration to get a desired outcome.

Chapter 3

1967-1971: Montini Catholic High School (Lombard, Illinois)

Freshman Year!

My first introduction to Montini, a Christian Brothers high school, was in the spring of 1967 at registration. My Dad came with me. He was a graduate of St. Leo High School, the class of 1943, and was taught by the Christian Brothers whom he greatly respected and admired. At Leo, if you got out of line, the Brothers could really let you have it! Corporal punishment was alive and well! After we signed a couple of papers, my Dad said to Brother Edmund, the founding principal of Montini, that *"if Jim here ever gets in hot water, you have my permission to give him what he has coming."* Brother Edmund just smiled (something I would never remember him ever doing again). I thought to myself, welcome to Montini High School!

Moving into high school for me was an exciting time but not without some trepidation. I can remember the nervousness I felt as a ninth grader! Puberty, as we all know kicks in at different stages for young adolescents. My voice had not changed, and I weighed a hundred and five pounds at five-feet, four inches! Some guys were already shaving, with deep voices, hairy legs and here I was still with freckles and a peach fuzz face! I did not have a growth spurt until my junior year when I finally shot up to six-feet, two inches.

Fortunately, those pre-puberty anxieties eventually went away, but when working with adolescents, educators need to be mindful that these thoughts are more on the minds of teenagers than the 3 R's.

The locker room and having to change in front of others for the first time can be a scary place.

The prior spring, before entering Montini, I took the entrance exam. Well, like every rite of passage exam I would ever take in my life, including the ACT and the Graduate Record Exam, I did horribly! Timed standardized exams have never been my strong suit! Later in my career, I would be an outspoken critic of standardized tests that, in my opinion, were used as exclusionary tools. More on this later in the book.

In the sixties and seventies, tracking and ability grouping students was alive and well. When I received my first schedule, there was not a foreign language listed. I was definitely in a cohort of students who like me, performed poorly on the entrance exam. We had different books and materials for the required courses of English 9, Algebra, and World History. Earth Science was substituted for a foreign language. After Christ the King and my minimal academic achievements in elementary school, I was pretty okay with my schedule. However, I was aware, that, like the old Hindu caste system, I was a *Shudra at the very bottom!*

I have often thought that Brother Edmund knew what he was doing when he assigned Coach Bill Pauls to be our Homeroom and World History teacher. He was a tough guy who was hired to primarily teach PE and coach varsity basketball. Our group of freshmen were the second class to enter Montini. The plan was to add a class each year until Montini finally had four grades 9-12. Pauls was a Physical Education major but Brother Edmund had him teaching our one section of World History. The other ninth graders were assigned to a scholarly social studies teacher.

Pauls was a star athlete himself at Mount Carmel High School and later at Lewis College in Romeoville, Illinois. In addition to coaching basketball, he was an outstanding football and baseball coach. Pauls could scare the hell out of us with his piercing eyes and deep voice, yet he connected with us in a way we knew he was our champion! You wanted to please him. Heck, we all knew we were in the lowest track, but he did not allow us to act like we were. He had high expectations.

Pauls had a winner's passion. When there was a Homeroom competition to see who could raise the most money for a Las Vegas fundraising gala, he pushed us to sell the most tickets and get businesses to buy the most ads for the program—and we did! He sold a lot of tickets himself, I didn't realize it then, but Pauls had no use for minimal achievers, whether it was in Homeroom or World History!

At semester there was a ninth grade World History exam competition. Pauls pulled several of us aside and very bluntly stated; *"I want you guys to study your asses off and do our homeroom and world history class proud."* Pauls taught strictly from the text that even had an accompanying workbook. He taught it cover to cover and would have test items that might touch on the most obscure passages. While his approach was simplistic and basic, it prepared us well.

I had the highest score in the freshman class. Five of the ten highest scores were Pauls' guys! It was only later that I realized Pauls himself may have had something to prove to his teaching colleagues and Brother Edmund! It wasn't that we loved history. We wanted to please Pauls because he believed in us! He gave us self-worth. We forgot about being in the lowest track, we now had confidence that we could flourish as high school students. Another great early mentor for me following Little League coach Bill Neuman.

For the first time in my life, I actually took academics seriously. I made the B honor roll and had A grades in World History and English. I remember bringing home the first report card to my dad.

I think he was in shock! I remember him taking the cigar out of his mouth and saying, *this is terrific Ace.*" My Mom was happy too.

As for sports, there was an announcement over the PA, the first or second day of school, stating that any boys who are not out for football must go out for cross-country if they expect to play on the basketball team. I was naïve enough to believe this! I could not wait for basketball to start in November! So, I went out for Cross-Country. Brother Andrew (pseudonym) was the coach. He had never been a runner, and you got the feeling that he was assigned the job because nobody else wanted it.

Brother Andrew would typically tell us to run this two-mile neighborhood course he had measured out in his car near Montini. Well, like most of the guys, after we were out of Andrew's sight, we would walk. When we finally finished, he would let us play pick-up basketball in the gym.

After a couple of weeks and the start of the season, I decided that maybe I should try to run the entire two-mile practice and not walk. After I did this for about a week, I started passing guys who were ahead of me in all the previous meets. I started to like it. There were two guys who had consistently been the top two finishers. By the end of October, I was beating both of them. All of a sudden, I was the best Cross-Country runner on the Montini team! I thought Holy Cow, maybe I can be good in this sport. I was not a sprinter, but distance running seemed a good fit. Even Pauls congratulated me in Homeroom, when he heard over the announcements I was our lead runner in our last meet of the season.

Well, cross-country was one thing, but basketball was my love. When tryouts came, I had a rude awakening. Over thirty guys tried out for the team. They divided the teams into an A and B squad. I barely made the A team. Coach Rich Hudik was the Freshman basketball coach while Coach Pauls handled the sophomores.

A lot of the guys, especially those who had played football in the fall, were a lot bigger, stronger, and faster than I was. I barely made the third string as a guard, but I was happy to be on the A team.

One of the things my Dad had a hard time grasping was the amount of time a high school athlete must dedicate to attending practices, including those on Saturdays! One of my chores in our household was to scrub the kitchen floor with Fels-Naptha soap every Saturday morning. I remember telling my DadI had basketball practice that I could not skip. He told me, "bullshit, you're scrubbing the floor, and tell your coach that on Saturday mornings you have home obligations." In his mind, school activities should be Monday through Friday!

I wasn't about to tell Coach Hudik that my old man was making me scrub the damn kitchen floor every Saturday morning. The following Monday when Hudik asked where I was, I told him I just forgot! That did not sit well with him. After practice he yelled over to me *"Fitzpatrick, get on the line"*. He made me run killers until I could barely walk. I threw up when I finally got into the locker room just barely making it to the toilet! When I got home, I told my Mom about it. She somehow talked my Dad into being a little more understanding.

As the season went on, I got very little playing time in games. I worked hard in practices and enjoyed being on the team. I was always on the traveling team, so I got to see all the schools in the Suburban Catholic Conference. I was beginning to realize that my career as a basketball player might end as a freshman.

After the basketball season was over, I went out for track in the spring. After cross-country season I got to thinking maybe I could be a pretty good two-miler on the track team. Coach Jim Kavanaugh the

Athletic Director was also the Track coach along with Coach Jim Mackey. My event was the 2-mile run.

By mid-season I seemed stuck in not being able to break the 12-minute barrier. On a cool overcast day in late May at Lockport West, I finally got under the barrier running a 11:43 two- mile! I still have a vision of Coach Kav running toward me with his stop watch in hand smiling and shouting *"you did it."* It seemed pretty cool to walk into the cafeteria and see the record Board: TWO MILE RUN: FITZPATRICK: 1968 11:43

On the social scene, one of the neat things I was experiencing at Montini and around the west side suburbs, were the dances on Friday or Saturday nights. My two favorite bands were *The Saints and Sinners,* and the *Jamestown Massacre.* These two bands played songs from the *Beatles, Blood Sweat and Tears, Three Dog Night, The Grass Roots, The Temptations, and The Fifth Dimension.*

At Montini, we would have *circle dances* where you didn't necessarily have to have a girl friend to dance. You just jumped in, tapped the guy on the shoulder you were replacing, and then got a few seconds to be in the circle with a girl until you got tapped out. They were so fun! Now and then, you would wait for a girl you had your eye on to jump in, and then you would jump in as well. It was even better if the girl jumped in after you, then you had a hint she might like you. Later on in the night, you might ask that girl to slow dance.

We had a dress code at Montini. Guys had to wear a shirt and tie, dress pants, dress shoes, and a belt. Girls wore skirts, blouses, and blazers. At dances, we got to see girls in mini-skirts, and we enjoyed that immensely!

During my Freshman year, a lot of things were happening in our country and the world. The Viet Nam war under President Johnson had escalated and there was major unrest on college campuses. The containment of communism policy was not working, and American soldiers were incurring mounting casualties every week.

The saddest event that I remember was on April 4, 1968, in Memphis, Tennessee. Dr. Martin Luther King was shot and killed on the balcony of a hotel. The Civil Rights Movement had been gaining a lot of momentum. Dr. King organized and led non-violent marches in many urban cities, including Chicago.

The news of Dr. King's assassination sent shock waves throughout the country! There was a violent and angry reaction to his death in every major city in the country. None worse than Chicago! Much of the west side of Chicago went up in flames with businesses being destroyed. Anger and racial tension was boiling over throughout our country. As the west side burned, I vividly remember the fear in my dad's eyes. My sister Maryann was in nurses training at Mount Saini Hospital on the west side of Chicago. I remember him bringing her home, taking an axe handle with him in case he was attacked.

I was too naïve and immature to understand the magnitude of what was really going on around me. We lived in suburban Lombard. It would only be later in my life, that I would truly understand the greatness of Dr. King and his legacy in the pursuit of social justice and equality. His efforts in the passage of the Civil Rights Act of 1964, in my opinion, make him the greatest American figure in the twentieth century. This act prohibited discrimination on the basis of race, color, religion, sex or national origin and its provisions forbidding discrimination on the basis of sex, as well as race in hiring, promoting and firing, might not have ever been enacted into law had it not been for Dr. King! In short, this legislation gave some hope that all could experience the American Dream. Now, many years later, there has been some progress toward equality, but not even close to where we ought to be as a nation!

On June 6th, 1968, one of the final days of my freshman year, our nation was struck numb again with the assassination of Robert Kennedy, the brother of President Kennedy. He was the leading Democratic candidate for the upcoming presidential election in 1968. He was running on a platform to end the Vietnam war and to move forward with the Civil Rights movement. I have always wondered, what could have been had he become president?

The women's lib movement was also a sign of the changing times. I was admittedly ignorant in understanding the magnitude and importance of this movement focused on equity and opportunity for women. I was under the impression that the father was the provider, and the mother was the caregiver. At fourteen and fifteen it never dawned on me that those roles could have been reversed. I certainly understand now, as a senior citizen, that your unconscious biases are often shaped by what you were culturally exposed to growing up.

I would have to chalk up my introduction to high school as a great success in my freshman year. Especially due to the influence of Coach Bill Pauls. A while back, I learned that Coach Pauls passed away January 10, 2019 after a long and courageous battle with cancer. One of my deepest regrets is that I never took advantage of the opportunity to reach out and thank him for the impact he had on my life. Today, as I teach aspiring school leaders I tell them to never procrastinate in thanking those who mentored and guided you into who you have become!

Sophomore Year!

Have you ever heard the expression the sophomore jinx? It's often mentioned in athletics when a player goes into a slump after demonstrating potential and success after a first year of competition. This is how I would describe my entire sophomore year and the first semester of my junior year.

As the sophomore year began, again Coach Pauls was our homeroom teacher and now he was charged with teaching a course entitled General Business. Again, no foreign language on my schedule and virtually the same classmates that were in World History.

I started the first couple of weeks doing okay, but then I stopped applying myself. Even Pauls noticed my decline and I got my first B grade from him. I also remember him pulling me aside and warning me that I might be hanging around with the wrong crowd. He was right I was! I was not applying myself in any classes.

In early November Coach Pauls shocked us in homeroom! He announced he would be leaving Montini by the end of the week. I could feel the tears in my eyes. How could he leave? Varsity Basketball was just around the corner, and we all knew Coach Pauls was looking forward to coaching the first varsity basketball team at Montini. I thought, God, he can't leave, he was our Homeroom champion!

We never knew the real reason Coach Pauls left. There were some rumors that he had a disagreement with the new principal, Brother Maynard (pseudonym). For the first time in my life, I was depressed. Even my parents knew Coach Pauls had a profound influence on me, and they were sad for what I was going through. I often wonder if I would have ever gone into education had I not crossed his path?

I was getting mostly C grades but some D grades in my courses. I slumped in sports as well, from being the number one cross-country runner to now barely finishing fourth or fifth on our team. When basketball season came around, instead of going out, thinking I would not get much playing time, I decided to work in a restaurant in the Yorktown Shopping Center. What a mistake! For me, my grades were always better when I was out for a sport. When track season came around, I did okay but not great. Academically, I barely finished my sophomore year with a 2.00 grade point average.

Sophomore year can be described in one word: *Bummer!* Reverting back to the vernacular of the day.

Junior Year!

Junior year did not start out much better for me. My grades were still suffering, and I was not working very hard in classes or on homework assignments. Mr. Locker (pseudonym) replaced Brother Andrew as the new cross-country coach. He was only marginally better than Brother Andrew. However, by now, I was understanding that I needed to motivate and push myself if I was going to improve. I began running on the weekends, and even getting up for early morning runs. I finished as the number two-man on the team behind Mike McLure (pseudonym). Mike was a sensational half-miler, and the star of our track and Cross-Country teams. He held the half-mile record for years after graduation.

By the first semester of my junior year, my grades overall were slightly improving. However, I did receive my first and only F grade in the second quarter in Physical Science, barely getting a passing semester grade of D. My Mom and Dad were not pleased. Science and Mathematics were never my strong subjects! I always performed better in social studies and English classes. Usually getting A or B grades in those subjects. I also received A grades in Religion class, which did not impress my dad. I remember junior year reminding him that I got an A in Religion. He said, *"you better get an A, why the hell do you think we send you to Montini?"*

Junior year, I noticed something else. We were no longer in academic tracks. I was in classes with some really sharp students. I was also now allowed to take Spanish. I was studying American Literature with students who were among the top ten in the class.

That made me feel pretty good, and allowed me to make some new friends.

One bitter disappointment for me was that my Dad would not let me get my driver's license until my eighteenth birthday. That would not happen until December 12th of my senior year. I tried like hell to get my mother to intercede for me, but unlike other times, she would not. How could a guy ask a girl out for a date if he did not have access to a car? I argued unsuccessfully that almost every junior had their license. I could always catch a ride to games and dances and to pizza places afterwards. However, my desire to date girls was really put on hold. I could have probably caught a ride and double dated for Homecoming and Prom, but I really wanted my license!.

As much as sports had dominated my high school experience, the highlight of my junior year was being involved in the Junior Variety Show. Our class moderator was a man named Mr. Jim Walsh, an English teacher. Mr. Walsh was a really talented guy. There had to be at least sixty to seventy students involved in this show, many of whom like me, were never involved in music or drama. There were a lot of athletes, and best of all, a lot of girls! Walsh by himself taught us to sing and even dance a little with show tunes from *Oliver* and *Damn Yankees!* Some of the skits were a riot with some of the funniest guys in the class doing a piece on *Snow White and the Seven Dwarfs!*

Back in 1969, there was a commercial for Diet Rite Cola, that featured Hall of Fame Boston Celtic's star, John Havlicek. He would come out and sing these lyrics; *"Yes sir, not on a diet, that's not why I buy it, it just got the taste that's right for me…Never had to get thinner, like it because it's a winner, just wish they'd change the silly name…What a waste, what a waste, when it's got the greatest cola taste! You there who ain't on a diet, will get no calories, just got to try it, just got the taste that's right for you"* While Havlicek is singing, he is doing this shimmy dance.

I got talked into being Havlicek. I shocked myself, that I had the nerve to do it. Everyone at the first rehearsal of this act laughed hysterically! They thought I did a pretty good imitation. Walsh said; *"Fitz you are in the show, don't change a thing."*

On the night of the show, my parents came. My Diet Rite cola act really caught them off guard. I had not told them about it. They thought I was great. There was standing room only in the auditorium. One other thing I remember from the show was a scene from the lyrics of the song *Hey Big Spender*. I had a beautiful girl, Cathy Brennan (pseudonym) who sat on my lap. After the show, my Dad said, *"I hope you got that gorgeous girl's phone number."* My smart-ass response was- *"yeah I wish I had my driver's license too."* That did make him chuckle, and he said, *"you only have a few more months to wait."*

I never had Mr. Walsh as an English teacher, but boy, am I indebted to him for what he did for me in that Variety show. In fact, I think this show brought the entire class of 1971 closer together. He gave me a chance to really build my confidence in front of a lot of people. Little did I know then, that in my career as a principal and superintendent, I would be speaking in front of large audiences in packed Board rooms or in over-crowded auditoriums, gymnasiums and football stadiums at graduations. How lucky was I to cross paths with Mr. Jim Walsh? I was starting to see a pattern here…Bill Neuman, Sister Carol, Coach Pauls, and Mr. Walsh had influenced me in wonderful ways.

Senior Year!

Senior year it was finally here! Tim Smith had decided that after his junior year at St. Charles Borromeo Seminary, he no longer would be seeking the priesthood. He would be coming to Montini. I was elated. For the past three years when he would come home on weekends from the seminary, we would hang out. He attended a lot of Montini events, so his enrolling senior year, was fairly smooth. He was reunited with several Christ the King classmates including Marc Weisenburger who would be his battery-mate the upcoming spring baseball season. He also knew Frank Harrison, another buddy, and Tim would become a really close friend with Mel Sego, another pal in our circle.

I got my class schedule, and now with math and science requirements out of the way, I really liked my classes with some social studies electives. I also would come to enjoy required senior courses, English with Sister Mary Jo, and Senior Social Studies with Sister Thomas Francis.

By the end of my junior year, I was a better than average distance runner, winning my share of races. There is that old saying, *"you don't know what you don't know."* Boy did I find that out! Coach Bob Hoppenstedt became my third Cross-country coach in four years.

Hoppy, as we referred to him, had a reputation for getting the most out of his runners. He came from nearby rival St. Francis of Wheaton, where he had great success. I had a huge growth spurt beginning my junior year and was now 6'2' and weighed almost 150 lbs. I was stronger, faster, and my endurance had never been better due to a lot of running during the summer. From day one Hoppy promised that in 12 weeks (the length of a fall cross-country season) we were going to run the best races of our lives if we stuck with him. He put us through some grueling workouts that resulted in several guys quitting. He challenged us until our lungs were burning!

For me the victories came in several dual meets. I was now the number one man on the team. I finished seventh in the conference meet earning all-conference honors. I set a new home course record at the Lombard Commons Park. Coach Hoppenstedt had instilled grit, toughness and most of all confidence in me. On meet day, I knew I was prepared to run a great race.

Montini held its first ever HOMECOMING in October of 1970. We welcomed our first graduating class back, the class of 1970. I had several friends and former teammates in this class. One of the really fun memories I have from that first Homecoming was the Friday night pep rally before the football game on Saturday. It was a raucous event to say the least led by Mel Sego, who was our spirit king! He had some great cheers that he would lead, including the famous chant of *Down by the River.* The whole class would respond and dance to his routine. What was neat about Mel, was that he was a loveable troublemaker at times. It was pretty neat to observe the faculty when he went into his act. They could only smile. Now and then, Mel would sneak in a dirty cheer at a game, that caught the ire of the game supervisors. He was the *God of the bleachers.*

Breaking school cross-country record at Lombard Commons Park in October of 1970, Coach Bob Hoppenstedt had me on the watch!

After cross-country season, I decided I wanted to go to St. Ambrose, and I wanted to teach and coach like Coach Hoppenstedt, a St. Ambrose alum. The drawback for me was my ACT score and my Montini transcript. My grade-point hovered around 2.00, not exactly what college admission officers were likely to view favorably. I had a discussion with my parents who by then understood the great respect I had for Hoppy, and I told them I wanted to apply to St. Ambrose University. I remember my dad, with the ever-present cigar, blew a little smoke and then asked me, *"Why St. Ambrose?"* I answered, *"that's where Hoppy went and if that was good enough for him, it sure would be good enough for me."* I can still remember my dad's response. *"I suppose that's as good a reason as any."*

Just before Thanksgiving, Coach Kavanaugh, who was also the guidance counselor, came to my first hour class asking the teacher to excuse me for a few minutes. He informed me that he was holding a copy of a letter that I would be receiving when I got home. St. Ambrose was not going to accept me until they had an opportunity to see my first semester grades of my senior year. Fortunately, I was applying myself and off to a pretty good start. For the next six weeks, I busted my butt, and nearly made the A honor roll for the first semester. Would that be enough to get me into St. Ambrose? Maybe too little too late! If only I had applied myself more sophomore and junior years!

Winter came, and now more than ever I was kicking myself for not sticking it out in basketball after freshman year. I played pick-up games with guys on the team, and I could hold my own now that I was bigger and stronger. However, coming off my most successful cross-country season, I had high hopes for the upcoming spring track season. Morning runs before school, and afternoon runs every day were now a part of my daily routines in the winter.

December 12th and my birthday came which meant I could now take the test for my Driver's License. I passed! On weekend's I would ask my Mom and Dad for permission to use the family car. I did not always get my wish, but when I did, I could now hang out with my friends and take my turn driving. Better yet, I could now ask a girl out for a date.

President Nixon was now president, and the Vietnam war was still going on with increasing casualties and unrest in the country. Many young men were fleeing to Canada to avoid the draft. I was eligible for the lottery draft, having turned 18 in December. College deferments were no longer being honored. My mother would tell me years later, that she never remembered a day when my Dad was so nervous. He knew what war was about. She remembered his phone call when my birthdate finally came up, around 260. He told her, *"Jim is safe, he won't be drafted."*

Years later, as I reflect back on this lottery draft day, it was so like my Dad to never let on what he might have been worried about, nor did he ever dwell or mention the sad and tragic things he endured in his life. His father died of heart failure when he was in eighth grade, and shortly after that an older brother Raymond, only fourteen, was killed trying to hop on a train. He also lost his mother shortly before I was born, and his oldest sister Kathryn, whom I vaguely remember as a toddler, passed away very young. Combine all these sad experiences and what he witnessed per the horrors of war, and it's only now that I appreciate the love he had for me and the anguish he would never want me to endure.

I was starting to really get worried about St. Ambrose. It was almost March, and I had not heard anything. Then one day, just like back in the fall, Coach Kav pulled me out of class again. He had a very grave look on his face, and I saw a letter in his hand. I thought oh shit, St. Ambrose rejected me. He then broke into a huge smile, and said; *"here is your letter from St. Ambrose welcoming you into their freshmen class of 1971—congratulations, now keep working hard this second semester on your grades."*

When I got home that day, my parents were really happy for me. My dad, looked at my Mom and said; *"I suppose we ought to take a ride to Iowa and check out St. Ambrose."* I will always remember that first trip to St. Ambrose with my Mom and dad, it was a special occasion, and afterward they treated me to a really nice dinner at the King's Palace, a high-end restaurant not far from our home. Now, the next challenge would be if we could afford it. My Dad was able to get me a great paying summer job at Wilbert Vault, where I mixed cement and made burial markers for Chicago land cemetery's. That, along with a national defense loan, allowed me to attend St. Ambrose.

My senior track season was pretty much cancelled after I hurt my knee in a toboggan accident that winter. A couple of years later I would have it surgically repaired.

In May I asked a really sweet girl, Mary Tokarski to the Prom. For a warm up date, I took Mary to a school play. When we arrived, I got out of the car and ran around to Mary's passenger side to open the door for her! I then slammed the door shut, catching my thumb in it! Damn, did it hurt, and I was too embarrassed and self-conscious to tell Mary just how much my thumb was throbbing. A couple weeks later, we went to the prom and had a very nice time. Mary looked beautiful, and it was my first time in a tuxedo.

My friend Tim Smith was off to a great start in baseball. He was the ace of the staff. Quite a success story having only enrolled in Montini his senior year. He was pitching great, leading our Broncos to victories. I remember seeing his Dad at one game at the Lombard Commons diamond, he looked so proud as he watched Tim take the mound! This was quite a contrast from a couple of months earlier.

Back in the winter, Tim decided to invite some friends to his house after a basketball game. Word of a party at his house spread like wild-fire through the bleachers. Tim did not expect his parents to be home before midnight. Surely there would be time to get everybody out of the house and clean up. Well, his Mom got sick, and they came home early. I can still see Tim's Dad and his red face as he walked in the door. He calmly said to Tim, *"I would like to park in my own drive way!"* There is an old saying, *"Someday, we will laugh about this, but it won't be anytime soon."* Over the years, we recounted this story many times.

In my experiences as a teacher, coach, and administrator in Iowa and Wisconsin, a negative regarding Montini was that it did not offer sports for women. Looking back, that was a real shame. I suspect we had some great female athletes in our class, if only they had the opportunity. My wife Therese, who I first met in college, would have been a great athlete if softball, basketball, and tennis had been offered for women. As my female classmates reflect back on Montini, I suspect some may harbor some resentment. If so, I sure could not blame them. My years in education have taught me that equity and inclusion, for all, not just some, is something our society must embrace.

I was elated to see at our 50th reunion how far Montini has come since its infancy years when I attended. There is now a full slate of interscholastic athletics for women. As we received a tour of the school, there were trophies, plaques, and huge portraits of women athletes and conference and state championship teams. This was nice to see!

We graduated in June of 1971. To this day our class of 1971 remains close even fifty-four years later. We have a couple of classmates who keep us informed about reunion gatherings and when someone in our class encounters adversity and needs our prayers. As I continue to write my reflections in this book, I continually see more clearly how experiences in those four years at Montini profoundly influenced me in my pathway to adulthood. Again, that spiritual underpinning that started in those early years of elementary school continued through high school without any of us ever realizing at the time, just how strong of a pull Faith is!

At the age of forty-eight I was selected into the Montini Catholic Hall of Fame, citing my athletic career accomplishments in high school and college and my professional accomplishments as an acclaimed high school principal. It was great to be a MONTINI BRONCO!

Summary thoughts and takeaways from this chapter!

- Pauls, Hoppy, and Walsh—what did they see in me that they invested their time and energy in bringing out my best? From our mentors, we learn to do the same for others in paying it forward, so we are influencers in the success of those we lead.

- Havlicek act: Sometimes we have to step out of that comfort level, even if it means doing something wild. It gives us courage and confidence to attempt great challenges in the future.

- The Drivers license: We don't always get what we want when we want it. A good lesson to learn early as it is likely to repeat itself time and again during our lives.

- Coach Hoppy: Grit can be learned, if we are dedicated and willing to make the sacrifices that success demands.

- St. Ambrose letter: every now and then when we are complacent we need a wake-up call to re-direct, motivate us and getting us moving forward.

Chapter 4

1971-1975 St. Ambrose!

There are times when I look back on my college years and they seem like a blur! I don't readily remember as many things from those four years as I seem to from my high school and grade school days. However, some of the most significant experiences that impacted my life happened in these four years!

The summer of 1971 was eventful in a couple of ways. In late August, I would be leaving home to attend St. Ambrose College (now known as St. Ambrose University). I was making really good money as an unskilled laborer with a wage of $4.50 an hour. Thank God and my Dad, for the job I had at Wilbert Vault, in Forest Park, Illinois! Along with my national defense loan, the job gave me enough money to afford room, board, and tuition.

At Wilbert Vault, I was mixing cement and making grave markers, working from 7 AM to 5 PM Monday through Friday. While I was grateful for the money, it was boring. I watched the clock, and the days seemed to drag on. I made a commitment to myself that for a career, I would never again hold a job where I had to punch a clock.

After work, I would get home by six, eat dinner, wait a half hour, and then go out for some long runs. My knee was holding up surprisingly well after my winter toboggan accident that had ended my senior year track season. My knee would lock or give out from time to time, but it generally held up. Coach Hoppenstedt knew Coach Roy Owen, track and cross-country coach at St. Ambrose. He was there during Hoppy's years on campus. He told me Coach Owen was a very fair man, and upon arriving on campus, I should see him right away about walking on to the St. Ambrose cross-country team.

I remember the day my parents dropped me off. My brother Kevin rode with us to Iowa. As they prepared to leave St. Ambrose, I remember my Dad telling me, *okay Ace, you are on your own, good luck, and he shook my hand.* My Mom had tears in her eyes and gave me a hug. Kevin looked sad, he was my youngest brother and only about ten at the time. I remember watching the car leave until it was out of sight. Then it hit me. Holy Cow, I really am on my own, with nobody telling me what to do, when to be in, or how to do things. And at that point, I did not know anyone. I thought all these years I yearned for more freedom. Now it seemed a little scary to have it!

St. Ambrose was a small Catholic liberal arts college in Davenport, Iowa, with an enrollment of approximately twenty-two hundred students. About half the students came from Iowa, while the other half came from the Chicago metro area and other parts of Illinois. There were also day students who came from the Quad-city towns around Davenport.

Many Chicago kids came from well-known Chicago schools like Fenwick, Leo, Brother Rice, and other suburban catholic high schools. It was a great mix of students. My first room-mate was a fellow by the name of Jerry Kelly from the tiny farming community of Castalia, Iowa, with about one-hundred and twenty-five residents. We got along great. We both went to bed early and got up early. I was saddened but not surprised when he decided to leave St. Ambrose after his first year. He had a girlfriend back home, and he missed her terribly. He would go on to marry her and become the manager of a lumber yard.

After the first day of college freshman orientation, I set out to find Coach Owen. I found his office near the old LeClair gym. The St.

Ambrose athletic facilities in 1971 were very outdated and in need of modernization. His office was very basic, but I remember seeing some really neat track and field pictures on the wall. I remember knocking on the door, and his voice welcoming me to come in. I told him; my high school Coach Bob Hoppenstedt recommended I see him about walking on to the St. Ambrose cross-country team.

Cross-Country teammates at St. Ambrose. Legendary Coach Roy Owen far left. I am third from left (Fall of 1975)

I remember Coach Owen looking at me before he began to speak. He had light colored brown hair and piercing blue eyes behind his glasses. He then said, I know Bob well. Practice begins next Monday. *"We work out twice a day with a morning run at 6:15 AM and afternoon practice from 3:30 to 5:30 PM. Does your schedule of classes work around these times?"* I said, Yes sir. He then told me to see Jerry Buttimer, a senior, who lived in Davis Hall. Jerry was the captain of the team and also made some side money as the team manager. Owen told me, *"Jerry will fix you up with some gear for practice, see you Monday"*.

I walked out of his office on clouds. I was going to get a chance to run in college. Jerry gave me two T-shirts, two pairs of running shorts, four pairs of socks, a blue pair of sweat pants, and a hoody, with St. Ambrose cross-country lettering. All of it was second hand and not in the best condition, but I didn't care, I was getting my shot.

The rigor of high school academics was one thing, but could I hack it at St. Ambrose and handle collegiate studies? After a month of classes, I found out I certainly could, and everything depended upon my applying myself and staying focused. Just about every night, Sunday through Thursday, I made it to the library and kept up on reading and writing assignments. My toughest freshman class was Spanish 201. After reviewing my high school transcript, they thought I could handle a two-hundred level Spanish course since I got A and B grades in my junior and senior years at Montini. The Spanish teacher was Father Dunne. He was very demanding in assigning work, and God help you if you did a lousy job. He had a nickname: *No Fun Dunne.* Believe me, it was well earned!

Father No Fun would typically assign exercises and passages for us to translate using the correct verb tenses and pronunciation. To his credit, he picked on everyone in the class, no one escaped his wrath that semester. You just always wondered when you walked into class if it was your day!

One day early in the semester, he called on me. For twenty solid minutes, he relentlessly berated me as I made one mistake after another, using incorrect verb tenses. He finally threw his book down and yelled; *"Fitzpatrick, I guess you can lead the horse to the water, but you can't make him drink it. Is there absolutely anything in this recitation that you think you might have gotten right?* I was embarrassed and responded angrily, *"probably not Father."* At that point I think No Fun sensed maybe it is time to lay off this guy, and he then moved on to another student.

After that humiliation, I never entered his class again without being well prepared. Mostly thanks to a classmate, Diane Mooney (pseudonym), a smart and sassy girl from Chicago who would meet with me the night before class in the library to go over what No Fun was going to cover the next morning.

One day, No Fun decided to pick on Diane, and he was getting on her really good with some sarcasm and comments. She abruptly began laughing and said; *"Come on Father this is college, do I really need to go to the Provost and report you."* No Fun was dumbfounded, and almost immediately moved on to another student. We laughed like crazy after class. No Fun never really toned it down, but he never called on Diane again. She got a final grade of A, and I got a B and was happy as a clam to receive it.

The first morning run practice with the cross-country team started out like a jog. It was a 3-mile run to Marycrest College and back. The last mile and a half was brisk, but I hung in there pretty well. The afternoon workouts would be very rigorous, often two-hour workouts. I found out pretty quickly just how much more strenuous collegiate athletics were going to be. It would be pretty hard to break into the top seven runners.

Our first meeting was at Wisconsin Platteville, I had a lot to learn. I finished ninth out of our ten guys. If I wanted to letter, I would eventually need to be in the top seven. After that first meet, I was not sure that would happen. By the end of a typical day of practice, I was pretty beat, but after dinner, I would force myself to go to the library and study.

By October, I was improving quite a bit. I actually started to finish fifth on our team in races. Part of the reason for moving up was that a senior, who was married, and taking classes just couldn't continue to commit to the program. Another guy just quit. Jerry Buttimer, was our most competitive guy who was always way ahead of all of us in practices and meets earning medalist awards at invitationals.

By the end of the season, I was consistently finishing in the top 5, earning me a college letter. I was thrilled when I was told to go down to Craton's sporting goods to get fitted for a St. Ambrose letterman jacket. Boy, I could not wait to go home at Thanksgiving wearing that!

While I was really enjoying college life, I missed home, and that is one of the things you learn when you go away, just how special home is. I was really looking forward to Thanksgiving. It was a three-hour drive from St. Ambrose back to our home in Lombard. My siblings always liked to point out that my mother would stock up on bacon before I came home on breaks. To this day, I love the smell of bacon and coffee, also remembering the aroma of my Mom's homemade bread. That first Thanksgiving, I came home with my St. Ambrose Letter jacket on. I could not wait to show it off to Coach Hoppenstedt and my Montini pals also home for Thanksgiving.

Early in my first couple of weeks at St. Ambrose, I met Nick Sigona and very quickly became close friends. He was on the varsity basketball team, recruited to St. Ambrose by legendary coach Leo Kilfoy. We often had meals together. Like me, he was fighting his way into intercollegiate sports. He was 6'7 and for his height, he had a great outside shot and spin moves to the basket. He played behind some bigger, stronger upper classmen, and only got limited minutes his freshman year.

Coach Kilfoy recruited him from Holy Trinity High School, where Nick attended his senior year. Nick was private about his life, but I later learned that for the bulk of his early years he was raised at Angel Guardian Orphanage (AGO). Nick was an inspiring guy. He had a car and often gave me a ride back and forth to St. Ambrose during the Holiday and semester breaks. My Mom loved to feed him! She also would send me care packages of chocolate chip and oatmeal cookies with a note to make sure that Nick got his package of cookies as well. By Nick's sophomore year, he was emerging as a star player.

Nick was not only tall, but also very handsome as well. While he was a star basketball player, he was a pretty good ladies' man as well! He dated a number of girls and a couple of them he dated steadily without either of them finding out, at least for a while. I didn't date much when I first arrived at St. Ambrose, just a couple of dates here and there.

It was not until I returned home for a Montini Homecoming in the Fall of 1971, that I met my first steady girlfriend. Her name was Allie (pseudonym). She was a Junior in high school, two-years younger than me. I met her at a sock-hop after the Homecoming bonfire and pep rally where she was a cheerleader. We dated steadily for two years going to concerts, Cub and White Sox games, the beach, movies, dances and summer festivals on the Chicago lakefront. She came up to St. Ambrose a couple of weekends.

In the Fall of 1973, Allie enrolled at the University of Illinois in Champaign, Illinois. That Fall when we didn't have a cross-country practice or meet on the weekends, I would hitch-hike down Interstate 74 from Davenport to Champaign. On a good day hitching, I could get there in three and a half hours. It was usually on a weekend when the Illini had a football game or there were some good weekend activities.

Out of the blue, in November of 1973, a guy knocked on my dorm room door and told me I had a phone call. Back then, there was a public phone on each floor, and whoever answered would let you know the call was for you. Well, it was Allie, and she told me her feelings for me had changed, and I should not come down to Champaign the following weekend as we had planned. I was stunned, really shocked, I did not see this coming at all.

Well, I stumbled back to my room and Nick bounced in as he often did, mostly looking to see if I had any of my Mom's cookies left over. Right away, he noticed the ashen look on my face and he said; *"what's the matter, you look like you saw a ghost."* Nick knew Allie, and understood how much I liked her. I told him about the Phone call I just received. He was ready to make a funny smart-alec comment on not getting so attached to a girl, but he thought better of it, seeing how crushed I was. He then grabbed me by the shoulders, and said; *"Fitz, you are too nice of a guy, she will regret dumping you, but just be glad there are guys around like me who even out the score! Let's go get some pizza and forget about this. You are going to find another girl who will treat you a lot better!"* At the time, I did not realize just how prophetic Nick's words would be!

Allie never really gave me a reason for breaking up. Maybe she was overwhelmed beginning college, or maybe her parents who I met up with on parents' weekend put some pressure on her to focus on her studies. Whatever the reason, I have learned in life that sometimes things just remain a mystery no matter how bad you desire explanations.

Only Nick could have made me feel better right at that moment. Although my thoughts lingered about trying to win Allie back when we would both be home for Christmas, it was not to be, despite my sending her flowers on her birthday in mid-November.

Lucky for me, I have always had a friend at a crucial time who could help me get through some things. Nick was that kind of friend. Following graduation, he went on to play a couple of years of professional basketball in Europe. Nick was inducted into the St. Ambrose Hall of Fame in 1987, having scored well over one-thousand points in his career.

So many years later, I am happy to report that Nick is very happily married to his beautiful wife Janis, who grew up on a farm in Minnesota, and they have two beautiful daughters. Nick defied the odds in over-coming many challenges and becoming a great success. He was the pride and joy of Coach Leo Kilfoy.

After my first year, I had to decide on a major course of study. I chose History, minoring in Physical Education, along with getting a coaching endorsement. I enjoyed World History, especially Greek and Roman history. St. Ambrose seemed like just the right fit for me. However, at the beginning of my sophomore year, my knee that I injured in the toboggan accident was becoming problematic again. It would give out and swell up. In October of 1972, I had a major reconstruction surgery with cartilage, ligament, and tendon repair. This wiped out my sophomore cross-country and track season. I hobbled along in two different casts for four months. Nick and Tom Lavin, another close friend, helped me out in getting to classes.

I spent the next several months working really hard to rehabilitate my knee in getting ready for Cross-Country, my junior year. By July, I was back, lifting weights and going on long training runs. The only downer was that Coach Owen retired from St. Ambrose. I wanted to show him I was back and ready to be the number one man on the cross-country team. He rewarded me with a sizable scholarship before he left. I had a nice Fall cross-country season under Coach Casey Simon (pseudonym), placing as a medalist in several meets.

Three months after my break-up with Allie, in January of 1974, I was in line at the library waiting to register for second semester classes. I noticed this girl in line who I had never seen before on campus. She was very pretty and had brown hair, brown eyes, a beautiful face, and a nice figure. She was dressed in jeans and had a brown coat on. I noticed a ring on her finger, and I was close enough to see the green stone and the words Alleman Catholic High School. Immediately, I knew she was a day student across the river from Illinois. We never said a word to each other, but we exchanged glances, and I detected a slight smile.

For the next couple of months, I never saw her again. Then in late March, there she was with some girlfriends in the campus pub. This time, I approached her and introduced myself, and learned that her name was Therese Kenney, in her first year of college. Our first real date was a walk in a beautiful park near the campus. We then stopped in the near-by Village Inn restaurant. I had just enough money to buy each of us a coke. From then on, our relationship developed. Soon after that, Therese would come to my track meets. I had recovered from my knee surgery and was turning in some of the best times of my life in the distance races I ran. On the side, I would make some money for dates with part-time jobs like helping a local painter or working the college switchboard during evenings.

Formal dance at St. Ambrose with Therese in spring of 1975

Therese was an excellent student and actually had earned an academic scholarship to St. Ambrose, but she still worked for extra money at a hospital. We went to movies, dances, Nick's games, and her parents often invited me over for dinner in Rock Island, where the Kenney's lived. Therese was also a sporty girl who loved the Cubs and knew quite a bit about all sports. During track season, I would often see her in the bleachers cheering me on. She smoked me the first time we played tennis. She was really good. Shortly after I met her, I knew she was the girl of my dreams, but we would have to wait until she graduated from St. Ambrose in the spring of 1977. This would also give me two years to get on my feet in starting a career, hopefully as a social studies teacher and coach, if I could find a job in education. Back then, good teaching jobs were not as plentiful as they are today.

When people reflect upon their college years, they usually are grateful for the career pathways their education provided them. I am thankful to St. Ambrose for preparing me to become a teacher and a coach. However, what I am most grateful for is not the education I received, but for offering Therese Kenney an academic scholarship! What a lucky thing for me to have crossed her path that glorious day in the library in January of 1974! I do believe the good Lord is always looking out for me, thus my deep faith! Thank you, St. Ambrose!

Summary thoughts and takeaways from this chapter!

- Sometimes we just need a chance to prove ourselves, nothing more: Thank you Coach Roy Owen, for letting me walk on to the St. Ambrose Cross-Country team in the Fall of 1971.

- No Fun Father Dunne: We need people to humble us every once in a while, they get our juices going and spark a better performance out of us.

- I often think of the Beatle song: *I Get By With A Little Help From My Friends:* Thank you Nick Sigona and Diane Mooney. Good friends are there when you need them the most!

- Sometimes we want explanation when there are none. Let go and move on!

- One heart-breaking experience, often paves the way for something spectacular to happen in our lives. Keep the Faith, and maybe a Therese Kenney comes your way!

Part 2:
A Labor of Love

Chapter 5

Beginning a career: Mason City Newman Catholic (1975-1980)

Many of my St. Ambrose classmates had secured their first career jobs before our graduation in late May of 1975. I had no such luck. I was hoping to get a job at Davenport Assumption High School, where I completed my student teaching, but there were no openings. A job in the Quad-cities would be great, as I would be close to Therese, whom I now had been dating seriously for the past two years. My Dad, always thinking ahead did secure my employment at Wilbert Vault for one last summer. The question for me was, what do I do come September?

In the seventies, there was a teaching glut, good jobs were hard to come by. I really wanted to teach and coach at the high school level, but any job at this point would be a blessing. I only had one interview in late June at a junior high in Naperville, Illinois. When I checked in for my interview appointment with the receptionist, there were five other candidates waiting on a bench who were competing for the same job! I didn't get the job. In a way, I was relieved, I wanted a high school job, but it was getting late.

In mid-July I got a call from Therese. She had a friend who worked in the St. Ambrose placement office who noticed a job opening at Mason City Newman Catholic High School in north-central Iowa. The job description looked like a perfect fit for me; teaching Social Studies with Cross-Country and Track coaching. Right away, I sent in my papers. A few days later, I got the call inviting me for an interview.

I had just bought a car upon learning that Wilbert would keep me on full-time after the summer if I was unable to secure a teaching job. That brought me some peace of mind, especially knowing that I could easily afford the car payments while paying my parents a minimal rent fee for living at home. I bought a brand new 1975 Chevy Camaro, no air-condition, but a nice-looking sports car for a guy 22 years old.

The interview at Newman High School was on a Saturday afternoon. It was approximately an eight- hour drive from Chicago. Therese and her family were kind enough to invite me to stay overnight that Friday night. That made the drive to Mason City on Saturday, much more manageable, about four hours. Therese accompanied me to Mason City for my 1:00 PM interview. We arrived in Mason City at about 12 PM. After a quick fast-food lunch, I dropped Therese off at a shopping mall not far from Newman Catholic High School.

Upon arriving at Newman, I was nervous. It was a very hot day. I had a shirt and tie on, and before I got out of my car, I did one last comb of my hair. As I shut and locked the car door, I realized my keys were still in the car! Well, nothing I could do about it then. It was 12:55 pm and I wanted to be on time.

The principal was Father John McClean, a very distinguished and handsome looking man with piercing eyes, I could see through his glasses. He had a genuinely nice smile. He greeted me warmly while introducing the athletic director and the social studies chair person. I interviewed with all three of them together and then with the social studies chair separately. Afterward, Father wanted to talk with me more and invited me to tour the grounds outside as he asked me questions pretty much related to my Catholicism and if I would be a good fit for this Catholic learning community that he led.

It was a nice campus, sort of out in the country. After circling the grounds and finally arriving at where my car was parked, Father ended the interview. I remember him telling me; *"Fitzpatrick, its between you and another candidate, and I have to think about it. The other candidate has teaching experience. You have the athletic and coaching background we are interested in. I will let you know my decision in a couple of days."* I remember looking him in the eye and telling him that sounded fine, and I really appreciated the opportunity to interview, and if chosen, I would work hard to do a great job. Then, I asked him if I could borrow a hanger from the cloak room in the outer office. I shared with Father that I accidentally locked my keys in the car when I arrived. He assured me that we could call the police to help me, but I insisted that would not be necessary if I could get a hanger.

We went back to the school office, where there was a closet with metal hangers. I grabbed one and headed back to my car. Unbeknownst to me, there was Father McClean following right behind me. He seemed interested in how I was going to get into the car. Well, Camaro's had these long front doors, so I really had to stretch the hanger to reach the lock button. On the very first try, it took me about three seconds to pop the lock. It was unbelievable. Father McClean, looked in amazement and said; *"That was incredible"* and his eyes looked the size of door knobs. Then I said; *it's not really a big deal Father, where I come from everybody knows how to do this."* He gave me sort of a look and I thought, oh crap, I just blew it. He probably thinks I am a crook!

A couple days later, I opened a letter and there was the contract for nine-thousand dollars to teach social studies and coach track and cross-country. I jumped for joy! Come late August, I would be heading to Iowa to become a teacher and a coach, no more punching a clock, and mixing cement!

First year teaching at Newman, just staying a day ahead of the kids!

First year teaching is challenging. Even strong young candidates coming out of college are going to struggle, especially with classroom management and curriculum pacing. I was no exception. Newman had fifty-minute class periods. I remember preparing my first lesson on the first day, and I was done in twenty-five minutes. What to do for the rest of the period? The kids sense when you are struggling, and while you don't want to be a yeller, they can push you with side-bar conversations and other behaviors where they are not engaged. I remember coming home tense and exhausted, just trying to keep up.

Hall of Fame basketball coach Al McGuire of Marquette University had a great quote; *"The best thing about freshmen is that they become sophomores!"* This is so true about teaching from your first year to your second year. It takes a little time to build your resources. Now, looking back after many years as an administrator, I believe it takes three-years for a teacher to become an emerging competent educator. It is in those first couple of years that a principal really has to support and mentor that young teacher. My second year of teaching would seem much more comfortable because now I had some experience.

During that first year, I got myself in a bit of a jam in mid-September. I had six guys on my cross-country team. The gear we had was in bad condition. I decided to buy my guys some nice grey cotton sweat suits with a hoody so they would look good at meets. I thought it would also bolster their pride as they wore them around school and town. The sweats cost me around one-hundred and fifty bucks, and I had them screened and lettered with NEWMAN KNIGHTS in cardinal red. About a week after the kids had them, one of my guys left his hoody on the bench when he went to take a shower. It was gone when he came back.

About a week later I was with two other young coaches at a bar-hamburger basket type of place. All of a sudden I notice a kid, a senior from Newman, wearing the stolen hoody! He see's me and with a buddy, heads to the bathroom. They come out and the other guy has the hoody on inside out. I was furious demanding the sweat shirt right on the spot raising my voice. Pretty soon, some of the patrons were upset with me making a scene. The coaches I was with convinced me to leave and deal with it on Monday at school. I was livid, I was only clearing five-hundred and forty dollars a month on my check. I wanted that stolen hoody back!

That Monday morning before classes, I had a note to see Father McClean in his office. What I learned was that Father knew the bar owner an alum of Newman who gave him a pretty detailed report on my outburst. As soon as I walked in, I noticed the hoody folded neatly on a side table. Father did not waste any time. He said, *"James, I have been so pleased with the job you have been doing both in the classroom and with the cross-country team. That was kind of you to purchase the sweats so the boys could have some pride in the cross-country program. Your passion and dedication are admirable, but you need to understand you represent Newman Catholic High School at all times when you are in the public. Now I believe in you, don't let anything like this ever happen again, have a good day, and here is the sweat shirt."*

Father McLean understood the art of using the *velvet hammer* with young educators who needed to be redirected and guided. He affirmed before he reprimanded me, thus making sure I knew he believed in me. These are the kinds of leaders you really learn from. They can convey with firmness the message you need to hear while keeping the relationship in-tact. This incident influenced me to have patience, understanding, but also high expectations when I would become an administrator.

By October of my first year at Newman, I was holding my own in the classroom, barely staying a day ahead of the kids. Coaching was different, it came naturally, largely due to the great mentoring I had from Coach Hoppy and Roy Owen. I understood how to train distance runners, and it was not long before this little team of mine started to round into shape. In our last meet of the 1975 fall season, we won the Eagle Grove cross-country invitational. Two weeks later, we finished 6th in the Class C small school class at state. I was surprised and elated with the success of the team. So was the entire school! At pep rally's we would really get pumped up, and I had a lot of fun leading the cheering for my guys!

My first coaching season in the fall of 1975 was a success. I was now done with coaching until the track season would begin in March, or so I thought! Before class began on an early day in November, Father McClean came into my classroom asking me for a favor. *"James, we are just beginning a girls basketball program, and we have a varsity schedule awaiting us. We need an assistant coach to assist Jackie Fisher, she can't handle the entire program by herself. I would like you to be her assistant!"*

First cross-country invitational win in October of 1975. We would go on to win the next 24 of 26 invitationals in the next four years.

First Newman women basketball team. Head coach Jackie Fisher on the far right. I am on the far left.

I was shocked. I knew nothing about women's basketball in Iowa, other than they played three on three, with three players (forwards) on the offensive end of the court and three players (guards) on defense at the other end of the court. I meekly mentioned to Father that I would really like to help, but I didn't know much about coaching girls' basketball. He was prepared for my answer, and said; *"I figured that since you came from Illinois, so here is the rule book,"* and he tossed it on my desk." *"By the way, practice starts a week from Monday at 6 AM. I would like to pay you, but there is no money in the budget for this position."* I vividly remembered my father once telling me that you never turn down a religious when they make a request of you. I assured Father I would take the job.

Jackie Fisher was an outstanding coach and, back in her day, a great prep basketball player from a small town about sixty miles from Newman. She knew the game and was a great strategist with outstanding practice and game plans for every opponent. We got better as the year went on, but our girls were just learning how to play basketball. We were playing a varsity schedule against girls who had been playing basketball since they were in early elementary school. We were losing by huge margins as we did one night in Osage, Iowa, a small town with a really good program. Even opposing coaches felt sorry for us, not trying to run up the score. Their reserves played a lot of minutes.

That night in Osage, I noticed Father McClean in the bleachers with another priest. I thought that seemed strange, he never attended road games. This was our last game before Christmas break. My Camaro back at Newman was all packed up. Upon returning from Osage, I planned to drive all night in getting back to Chicago. After a semester of teaching and coaching, I was anxious to celebrate Christmas with my family. As the game ended and I was walking off the court, Father McClean called out to me. He asked me to meet with him shortly after Jackie and I met with the team in the locker room.

As I walked to the locker-room, I thought, "oh my what did I do?" I was a pretty rough edge. Did I say something profane or inappropriate? It was possible. I could let some words slip now and then, but I thought I had been careful, especially after the hoody incident. Was I in hot water?

When I returned to the floor, Father McClean reached into the lapel pocket of his black suit coat and pulled out an envelope. I opened it, and there was a short note thanking me for coaching the girls, along with his personal check for fifty dollars. He said, *"I understand you're driving to Chicago tonight, maybe this can help with some gas and coffee!* He even told me where I could cash it at a nearby gas/food mart close to Newman. He smiled, said Merry Christmas, and walked away. Upon reflection, I have cashed a lot of big checks in my career, but none ever seemed more meaningful than this one! He didn't have to do this, but he did. Not only writing the check, but also making the trip to Osage. I think gratitude and affirming people were valuable lessons I learned from Father McClain.

Following Christmas break, we continued our losing ways until one night in early February, we defeated Bancroft St. John's in a close game at home. They had defeated us in their gym earlier in December. When that buzzer went off, I jumped for joy, picked Jackie up in the air, and shouted to the student cheering section who had been enthusiastically cheering for us, to meet me and the team at Pizza Hut, we are going to celebrate, and I am buying! My passion and exuberance had over-taken me. When I got to the locker room, it dawned on me, how many of these kids are going to show up at Pizza Hut? Well, about two-hundred dollars' worth of pizza later, I had my answer, but what fun it was to have this spirited moment. After seventeen straight losses, we finally got a victory!

At the end of my second year at Newman, Therese and I got married in Rock Island, Illinois, at St. Pius X parish on June 11, 1977. Father McClean had known about our engagement and attended our wedding. Earlier that fall, he called me into his office. He asked me if I had ever considered going into school administration. Up to that point, I had not, but I was well aware that making ends meet on a teaching salary would be tough for Therese and me, especially when we started a family. Therese would be looking for a Spanish teaching job.

Wedding day, June 11, 1977 at St. Pius X Catholic parish in Rock Island, Illinois.

Father needed a Dean of Students for the following year, and he wanted to appoint me. He thought it might be a good experience for me to enroll in the University of Iowa educational administration program. He suggested I talk it over with Therese, and consider registering for classes that summer. So that's what we did, and I started classes the week before we got married, delaying our honeymoon until August when classes would be over. For the next three summers, we would sub-let an apartment in Iowa City, where I eventually earned my Master's Degree in Educational Administration in the Summer of 1980.

Wedding day – my wonderful in-laws Henrietta and Ed Kenney in the middle, Therese's siblings, Joe, Mary, and Tom.

Beginning my third year at Newman, now married, I began my new role as Dean of Students and part-time social studies teaching. I continued to coach cross-country and track, and now became the sophomore boys' basketball coach. It was a busy year. We rented a small apartment and struggled with the monthly bills, but we made it with Therese taking on a couple of part-time aide jobs in nearby school districts, while still looking for a full-time teaching job.

Parents of my cross-country and track teams were very kind to us, inviting us for dinners, or social get togethers after games. One family, the Mataloni's seemingly adopted us. Their son Tom was a star cross country and track runner who captained our teams.

With my coaching schedule, we could not get home to our family's during Thanksgiving or Easter, and Henry and Tula Mataloni always hosted us on these holidays, looking after us like surrogate parents. They drove Therese to many of my cross-country and track meets and basketball games. They would come by our little apartment with ice cream sundaes. They were so good to us! There were others as well, like the Karamitros, Cahalan, Bernemann, and Pirkl families, who extended so much kindness to us. The same with the Presentation Sisters, who were the Newman nuns, becoming close friends and were great mentors to me during my first couple of years of teaching. Those are the things you cherish when you think of past relationships and the people who helped you along the way.

State champion picture of Newman Knights in 1979, I am on the far right, Sister Beth Kress, my assistant, is in the third row to the left.

The year 1979 will always be memorable. It was my fourth year at Newman. Therese was pregnant. Tula Mataloni would call Therese every morning to see how she was doing or if she needed anything. We had so much support, and the parents of all the runners had a baby shower for us. On the afternoon of January 24, our daughter was born. Therese had been up all night and went through a very difficult labor. Finally, at 1 PM, Megan was born. I had left the hospital to call my mother-in-law first about the news, and then my family. I also went back to Newman to stick celebratory cigars in everybody's mail box. It was then that my friend and the counselor Craig Ghinazzi informed me the hospital was trying to reach me, and I had better get back there right away. Therese was having complications.

Our regular doctor received news the previous night that his father had passed away. However, he left word that if Therese Fitzpatrick went into labor, he was to be called immediately. Somehow, the message did not get through the channels at Mercy Hospital, and he had left town. A resident, not an obstetrician, had been working with Therese through the delivery. Therese was hemhoraging, and he and the staff were struggling to get her stablalized. When I got back to the hospital, the room seemed crowded, with even the Chaplain. I thought oh My God, this can't be happening.

A few minutes later, a gynecologist in his scrubs rushed in (Dr. Smith -pseudonym). It was like a parting of the sea, with everyone getting out of his way. He repaired her ruptured cervix and stopped the hemohriging, which required her needing six units of blood. Ironically, Dr. Smith had been called out as public enemy number one in the Catholic community because he performed abortions, and here he was saving my wife's life.

After twenty minutes, Dr. Smith came out of the operating room, and into the crowded waiting room filled with nurses and hospital people. I could see he had a little sweat on his brow, and I could tell he was looking for me. He eventually spotted me and said; *"Mr.*

Fitzpatrick, your wife is going to be just fine, and you have a beautiful little baby girl. God bless," and he immediately began to walk out before I chased him down, shaking his hand and thanking him. I could not hold back my tears of joy. What an ordeal, one minute you are on the top of the world, and the next minute you are about to lose the love of your life! We celebrated that night in the hospital room, where they prepared a nice dinner for new parents. We took turns holding our new bundle of joy-Megan.

Any time after that day when I heard somebody express anything negative about Dr. Smith, I would cut them off and say, well, I have another story to tell you about him, and how he saved my wife's life.

In addition to Megan being born in our fourth year in Mason City, the year was memorable for another reason. Father McClean had left Newman to become the pastor of a parish in Marion, Iowa, after the 1977-78 academic year. Our new principal was Father Ken Gehling, a wonderful man with a big heart and a hearty laugh. Father McClean would be a tough act to follow after his tenure of over ten years. As his Dean of Students, Father Gehling was a joy to work with, and always very supportive of me with some of the really tough disciplinary decisions I sometimes had to make.

I stayed at Newman for five years. Longer than I had ever imagined. I thought initially I would get a year or two of experience, and then Therese and I would move to either the Chicago suburbs or the quad-cities to find jobs. As it turned out, I loved Newman. The faculty, staff, students, and families meant so much to me.

As a teacher, I was getting better every year. I remember the diocesan superintendent of schools observing me, and afterward, he told me, nice job, you really have rapport! Along with my teaching improving, the real pull for me in staying at Newman was that I promised the entire school that our cross-country team would win the school's first ever state championship. I simply could not leave until this was accomplished. I was driven to this end. To this day, I will always love and appreciate Therese for knowing what this meant to me. We were living from paycheck to paycheck, so staying at Newman was quite a sacrifice on her part.

That Eagle Grove invitational victory, that first year, was the start of a tradition at Newman. Over the next five years, we won twenty-four of twenty-six invitational meets while not losing a dual meet. We became a perennial cross-country power in the state of Iowa.

Tula and Henry Matalon were adoptive parents for Therese and me during our years in Mason City. Theron Son Tom captioned the 1978 team.

After finishing runner-up in the state cross-country meet in November of 1978, our goal in the fall of 1979 was to win the state crown. We started off that September with a bang, winning six straight invitationals and going undefeated in dual meets as we entered the second week of October. Then adversity struck! One of our best runners was still recovering from a staph-infection that nearly took his life the previous winter. However, he had recovered, but now was having a setback. Another one of our top runners sprained his ankle.

Pep rally at Newman to fire up crowd before state meet.

Going into the district meet in Waverly, Iowa, we had to finish in the top four to qualify as a team for the state meet. We limped in, barely qualifying with a fourth-place finish. Our reserve runners came through! In the two previous years, we were district champions, and now we were barely hobbling into the state meet. We had two-weeks to heal and get healthy.

Al Michaels, the famous broadcaster, will always be remembered for his call of the USA victory over Russia in the Olympics on February 22,1980, when he shouted in the last seconds of the game, *"Do you believe in miracles?"* Well, I do believe a miracle occurred on November 4, 1979, in Ames, Iowa, the site of the Iowa State cross-country meet.

After barely qualifying for the state meet, I was pretty resigned to just being happy that we qualified for the state meet. The state crown that looked so promising in early September seemed like a fading dream. We were feeling better, and I had my top guys back in the line-up, but it seemed like an unreasonable expectation to think they could even place in the top five.

The starting gun went off, and after the first the mile, I was amazed to see that our guys were holding their own. Then, when it came to the second mile and the last four-hundred yards, all of our guys were sprinting, finishing strong, passing other competitors. A sophomore who never finished higher than fifteenth in our previous invitational meets finished in eighth place. How in the world did he pull this off? Our number one man finished second overall, and we placed four guys in the top twenty to win the state championship!

State champions, top five runners in the Fall of 1979.

To me, that was a miracle. I don't think any team coming out of districts as a fourth-place qualifier has ever come back to win the state championship. God was good to us that day. Mission accomplished- the first state crown for Newman Catholic High School. At the victory reception at Newman the next day, one of the runners was asked what inspired you guys to win the meet? His response was that the principal, Father Gehling, after the pre-race prayer, told us to run like hell! For me, this race signified the end of my time at Newman. I was now free to move on to the next phases of my career, I had made good on my promise. I was now anxious to take the next step into school leadership, in seeking a principal job. The following summer, I would attain my certification and Master's Degree in Educational Administration.

The Kenney family photo

Sometimes I think back on how lucky was I to start my career at Mason City Newman. Just imagine if Therese's friend had not thought of me when she first saw that Newman vacancy in the St. Ambrose placement office! To this day, winning the State Championship in the fall of 1979 is one of the top highlights of my life. It was also a turning point for me. I now realized that with God's help and inspiration, I could lead, motivate, and coach people into achieving worthy organizational goals. Little did I know what the future would hold as I took my career to the next level of school leadership.

More than ever, I believe the good Lord is always looking out for me!

Some thoughts and takeaways from this chapter:

- The lucky call from the placement office friend to Therese: Do we ever think back and appreciate the lucky breaks we get in life.

- As we move through life, we find new mentors like Father McClean and Father Gehling who have the patience and understanding to allow us to mature and grow.

- The velvet hammer: For a leader, it is possible to re-direct behavior while keeping a relationship in-tact.

- Newman Girls first varsity victory: Celebrate even the small wins when you are going through challenging times.

- Dr. Smith: never write someone off before you get to know them or see them in action for yourself.

- State championship: never give up on your dreams. Believe in miracles-they happen!

- Good leaders always know how to express their gratitude to others.

Chapter 6

Early Principalships In Iowa (1980-1986)

Following the state championship at Newman, the following spring of 1980, I was busy looking for an entry position into high school administration. By August, I would be fully certified as a principal with my degree from Iowa. My priority was to land a job as an assistant principal in a large high school. However, there were not many opportunities.

In early May, I interviewed for the junior and senior high school principalship in Lost Nation, a tiny town in eastern Iowa. The enrollment in grades seven through twelve was one-hundred and forty-three students. Pretty small, but I had to get a start somewhere. The school was only three hours from Chicago and only forty-five minutes from Therese's parents in Rock Island, Illinois. That appealed to both of us, after having lived so far away from family while in Mason City. We were elated when I got the word that I was selected.

My salary was now twenty-three thousand dollars, more than Therese and I were making combined in Mason City. Therese, too, would seek a Spanish teaching job, which she landed in a small community near Lost Nation. With our new combined income, we could now do more things and save some money for eventually buying a home. We did not want to be renters the rest of our lives. Megan was not quite yet two. We also knew this was a stepping stone job, hopefully to more opportunities in the future.

Prior to our moving, Therese's Mom and Dad found us a nice house to rent on a farm. Lost Nation was not far from Clinton, Iowa, where Therese's Dad was from, and he had relatives in the area. The day we moved in, Therese's family was there to help us, and the superintendent and several faculty members greeted us as we pulled in, helping us unload the moving van. Such a kind, welcoming gesture. Later that night, one of the teachers had us over for dinner.

Masters degree from Iowa with Mom and Dad

Moving to a small rural community was quite an adjustment for Therese and me. We adapted and really learned a lot in the two years we lived in this community. The superintendent, Bob Steele, was a sharp and savvy guy. He understood the politics of a farming community and knew how to leverage his influence. I learned quite a bit from him. It was my first introduction to public school governance. Bob was good at it; he knew how to stretch a dollar!

Initially, the job posting and description was for the Junior-Senior High School Principalship. Well, the job entailed a lot more than just that. I was also the athletic director and required to teach eighth grade American History. I cannot really complain, because upon coming to Lost Nation, I still was hoping I could do a little coaching.

As I began, I tried to remember and emulate many of the leadership practices I had observed in Father McClean and Father Gehling, along with what I had learned in my administration classes at Iowa. While this helped, there are just a lot of things you have to learn on your own. One of the things I realized later, is that I really

did not know how to delegate and effectively use the skills of an administrative assistant (then called a secretary). As a rookie principal at twenty-six, how do you gain the trust and followship of veteran teachers? Well, I did okay with the trust, because they were tolerant of my rookie mistakes.

A highlight of my time in Lost Nation was coaching. Shortly after arriving, I got permission from the Superintendent to start a cross-county program for boys and girls. What I learned is farm kids are tough and know how to work hard. They learn to be responsible in being assigned farm chores at an early age. They naturally took to distance running.

By October we ran in a few dual meets, got entered into the districts, and we qualified both the girls' and boys' teams for the state meet in the small school class. The boys finished third in the state. In our second year, we got bumped up a class and were assigned to the same district as Newman. We lost the district championship by one point to Newman! Three of those Newman runners were holdovers from my state championship team. We advanced to the state for a second year. With the boys finishing sixth and the girls eleventh.

The Lost Nation job was really a great learning experience. It was a very demanding job. I had to learn how to do a little bit of everything from making the Homecoming queen's tiera out of aluminum foil, to sitting with the superintendent at the collective bargaining table. I also had to learn how to develop a master course schedule. Not easy in a small school where you have a lot of single section classes and half-time shared teachers with nearby school districts. I had my first introduction into budgeting although the superintendent guarded that pretty closely for which I was grateful. I learned a little bit about recruiting and hiring teachers and coaches, along with hiring game officials for sports, and arranging transportation and supervision at events. I was expected to be at all games, concerts, and all junior-senior high activities. I also had my introduction into observing and evaluating teachers and staff.

The most difficult challenge for me emotionally was making the transition from being a teacher/coach to becoming a school administrator. I had experience redirecting student behavior at Newman as the Dean of Students, but this was different. At Newman, I was a popular young teacher/dean, and coach, enjoying the accolades of students, parents, and peers. When I had to deal with suspensions or athletic training rules in Lost Nation, some people were not only unhappy with me, but down-right angry and vindictive. It was also my first true experience of inadvertently making enemies!

While I was respected by the majority of students, parents, staff, the superintendent, and the Board, I was sensitive to those who didn't care for me. It really impacted me mentally. Our lawn was trashed on a few occasions, and a swing set we had set up for our three-year old daughter Megan was totally torn down and demolished. In short, living out in the country was scary, and at times, I stayed up looking out the window, worrying someone would do more damage to our property. There were no police, just the county sheriff's department making passes on the highway we lived on. One night at a Board Meeting, and angry parent suddenly came storming in. His son, who was a member of the cross-country team had the tires on his car slashed. When we went out to the parking lot, my tires were slashed as well. Not a good night.

My siblings starting on the left–Kevin, Jeannie, Tony, Therese, Maryann, Annemarie, and Kathryn (KK). Mom seated in front.

A highlight of my time in Lost Nation was helping a student get admitted to Notre Dame. We had a skeletal curriculum without AP and rigorous college prep courses. We barely could offer chemistry, physics, and trigonometry. When he got his acceptance letter we made a copy of it and posted it on the four corners bulletin board. The Notre Dame stationery was beautiful with gold and blue trim, welcoming our young man into the Notre Dame freshman class of 1981. Another highlight for Therese and me was chaperoning the junior and senior class trip to Washington DC. This was a wonderful experience for many students who had never traveled or been far away from Lost Nation.

After two-years we were ready to look for another principal position, hoping now I could advance to a larger high school. In April of 1982, our wishes would come true. I was selected to become the Principal of West Liberty High School (WLHS) beginning the following fall.

Following my announcement to the Lost Nation Board that I would be resigning, I heard through the grapevine that after services at the Lutheran church, a comment was made that the Board should never hire another catholic principal again. I thought, wow, that is the first time I ever heard my faith being held against me. It really resonated with me and opened my eyes to be more vigilant in recognizing the discrimination and the prejudice that some people have to endure. It emboldened me to make sure that in my leadership, I would never tolerate prejudice or bias, unconscious or deliberate! Another takeaway was to always salvage relationships with students and parents when conflict arouse. I got better at this later in my leadership roles.

I left Lost Nation grateful for the experience and thankful to the superintendent, faculty, and staff who endured my growing pains. They were kind in acknowledging the positive energy and spirit I had infused into the school. At the last Board meeting, each member complimented me on doing a great job, expressing their regrets that I was leaving, but wishing Therese and me the very best. Superintendent Bob Steele, in his reference letter to West Liberty, no doubt carried a lot of weight in my being hired. One more mentor crossing my path, who taught me a great deal in two-years.

So, it was on to West Liberty, Iowa, in the summer of 1982. Therese and I arrived in July, renting an upstairs apartment from Joe and Priscilla Hessig, who were very good to us. This time, the job was indeed the principalship, I was relieved not to have athletic director duties. I was now twenty-eight, with still a lot to learn about school leadership.

My new boss was Del Jeneary. He had been superintendent in West Liberty for many years. I really liked him a lot. He could be gruff, but he was always straight forward with me and very supportive. Within a month of school starting in the fall of 1982, I had the impression that Del just wanted me to run the high school and let him know if there was anything I needed. I don't think Del set foot in the high school more than ten times during my four-year tenure. He was a hands-off superintendent who expected you to do the job. I knew from other principals in the district he could have a temper if you messed up, but with me, he was always supportive.

Finally, homeowners in West Liberty, Iowa Fall 1980

After a few months, Therese and I bought our first house, a two-story stucco home on Calhoun street in West Liberty. A short walk from my office. To us, this house was like a castle. After being married five years, we finally had a home. It didn't take long for Therese to spruce it up. Both inside and out! We had a really nice porch, and Therese had hanging plants and flowers, really giving our house a beautiful curbside appearance. My mom always marveled about Therese's ability to make a house a loving home! She would do this at every stop and house we would live in.

The previous principal had incurred a severe stroke, a real shame as he was near retirement. I felt bad for him and would visit him from time to time, he had been the principal for many years. It was hard for him to communicate as his speech was severely impacted by the stroke. He would try to write things down for me when he really wanted to get his message across.

A very pivotal person to impact my life when I arrived at West Liberty High School (WLHS) was the long-time school secretary, Mrs. Celia Bjork (fondly known as Mrs. B). She was so good in her role. Her knowledge of the high school, the district, and the community would be so helpful as I began my tenure as principal.

When I came into the office for the first time on July 1st, 1982, she was already finishing up the master scheduling. It was in this job I learned just how a secretary (or an assistant) could be such an asset to you. She knew how to receive people on the phone or in the office, and her typing was impeccable, which was before word processing! In short, she really looked out for me and often warned me of an issue that was coming up before I realized it. I remember the athletic director, Greg Guinn, telling me Mrs. B could run the school if you let her. The neat thing about Mrs. B, is that she wanted me to be the leader of the school and supported me in every way she possibly could.

Greg Guinn, the athletic director, was also a great influence on me. He was a straight shooter, honest, and ethically sound. Greg often projected a very serious demeanor. He was a ruggedly handsome guy who grew up in Nebraska. In addition to being and excellent Business Law teacher and athletic director, he was a great coach, especially in golf, where he has been inducted into several state and national Hall of Fames.

During my four-years at WLHS, Greg was my closest confidant. He and his wife Debbie and their two sons had lived in West Liberty for a long time. Whenever I had a big decision to make, I would confer with Greg to get his opinion. A good example was when we went through a North Central Accreditation (NCA) review. Back in the 1980's this was a really important process, and you wanted to be reviewed favorably. After the self-study portion, I was surprised at how critical the staff was of the facilities and resources. I remember telling Greg; *"I don't want to even show this to Del (the superintendent), he's going to blow a gasket!"*. In no uncertain terms, Greg said, *"You march this report right over to him. Del needs to know he and the Board have neglected the high school for too long. It's high time this district gets busy figuring out how we can deliver education in more updated facilities. Just take a look at West Branch (our neighboring school district), which just built a new high school."* I followed Greg's advice, and predictably, Del was not too happy, but the reality was evident that our facilities not only needed to be refreshed, but we needed to build a new high school, but which did not happen until many years later.

Another issue where I appreciated Greg's support was when it came to athletic conference realignment. In 1983, I was president of the then Eastern Iowa Hawkeye Conference (EIHC), where principals served as the Board of control and the presidency was rotated among the eight-member school principals. Iowa City Regina, where Therese was a Spanish teacher now in her fourth year, was requesting to get into the EIHC conference along with near-by Tipton High School. From my days at Newman, I knew what it was like to be independent and struggle to find a full slate of games to complete a schedule. The fear was that catholic schools without boundaries could recruit and have an unfair athletic advantage. Thus, it was difficult for them to gain entry into a public-school athletic conference.

There was a lot of resistance to the Regina joining our conference. My question was, then, why do we and other schools in this conference have them on our schedules for non-conference contests? Five of the eight schools played them in boys' and girls' basketball, and a couple of others, like us, played them in football.

Our popular veteran varsity basketball coach was vehemently opposed to Regina joining the conference. Greg, in addition to being the athletic director, was also the assistant varsity basketball coach. I had met with the Regina principal a couple of times, and I really understood how he was trying to resolve the long road-trips on week nights especially during the winter sports season when roads could get pretty bad. His kids, on school nights, would often not get home before midnight. Eventually, some of the EIHC principals were becoming more accepting of Regina joining the conference. The West Liberty vote would be crucial, and no other varsity coach was more opposed to accepting Regina than my coach, whom I liked and deeply respected, even in disagreement.

A couple of days before the crucial vote, Greg came into my office and shared that we should vote to approve Regina's entry into the conference. This was a brutally difficult decision for Greg, given his relationship with the varsity coach. Upon learning West Liberty would vote for Regina and Tipton to be admitted to the conference, all seven other schools voted unanimously to accept them into the conference.

Following the decision, our varsity basketball coach announced that he would be resigning his coaching position, even after our team made it to the state tournament. There was no doubt that his decision was based on his belief that Regina would dominate the EIHC in boys' basketball and recruit players from West Liberty and other conference schools close to Iowa City. Well, that never did come to fruition, as there was competitive balance when it came to conference championships.

Maybe the best lessons I learned in coming to West Liberty was to really appreciate all of the academic offerings and departments. West Liberty really had some gifted teachers in all of these areas. My strength coming into school administration mostly came from my social studies and coaching background. Thus, in Lost Nation, my attention, due to inexperience, was focused more toward athletics than music.

Del Jeneary was pretty much a hands-off superintendent, except when it came to music. He encouraged me to really be supportive of music. The show choir known as *Black Satin* was really outstanding and well-known in Iowa music circles. For years, they had performed well and had sent audition tapes to the *Bishop Luers Midwest Show Choir, in Fort Wayne, Indiana.* This was like the super bowl of show choir festivals, and every year, the hard-working choir director would receive a disappointing letter informing him that Black Satin didn't make the cut for the festival. However, in the winter of 1983, the choir director came bouncing into my office, waiving the Bishop Luers invitation for our show choir to compete. I was overjoyed for him. He and his music kids had worked so hard. At long last, *Black Satin* was in the Bishop Luers festival!

Our excitement almost immediately hit a speed bump. Fort Wayne was eight hours away. The audition time was set for eight o'clock on Saturday morning, our boys basketball team had a home game that Friday night. It had been a rough winter with lots of snow. Three of the boys in Black Satin were also members of the varsity basketball team. Two of them were starters, and the third was like the sixth man. The show choir director wanted them excused from the basketball game, and the varsity coach thought that was an absolutely absurd thought, that these guys would miss a varsity basketball game for a show choir competition. This was good preparation for the many dirty dilemma's that I would face in my career.

I came up with a plan. After the varsity game, which would end at about 9 PM on the Friday night, I would drive the three guys to Fort Wayne. If the roads were bad, we would not make the trip. Del agreed to my plan, although he was really angry with the coach. I remember him quipping; *"why the hell can't they miss one game for cripes sake."* Although, as I recall, his language was a little more colorful. The coach did not like the plan at all, he thought it was a distraction, after all this was a varsity conference game. The choir director was pleased his show choir would be at full strength, although he was unhappy his three guys would miss the Friday practice rehearsal in Fort Wayne where the choir would arrive on Thursday night in advance of their Saturday performance. Compromise is not always easy to arrive at, but everyone had to give a little. As luck would have it, the basketball team won, and I arrived with the boys in Fort Wayne at 7 AM, in time for our show choir to perform at 9 AM. I remember helping the one fellow get into his outfit. They performed well and made the finals!

West Liberty was a town of twenty-seven hundred residents. While I did not think that driving to Fort Wayne would get much attention, I was surprised. I received several notes thanking me for understanding just how important it was to the boys that they not miss this festival, feeling I went well beyond the call of duty. After my West Liberty experience, my takeaway was that all student activities would be valued, not just sports. I have Del Jeneary to thank for that.

By the winter of 1986, in my fourth year as principal of West Liberty High School, I was once again ready for a change. After moving to West Liberty, I resumed my graduate studies at the University of Iowa, earning credits beyond the Master's Degree. Dr. George Chambers was my advisor, and another great influence in my life. He encouraged me to pursue a superintendent license and an

Educational Specialist Degree, a midway benchmark to a Doctoral degree.

In the spring of 1986, Del Jeneary announced his retirement, effective at the end of the school year. While my goal was to secure a large high school principalship, those jobs seemed hard to come by in the state of Iowa unless you were already a large high school assistant principal, well-groomed to move into the role!

Upon receiving my Iowa superintendent endorsement, I applied to succeed Del for the superintendent job in West Liberty. I also had some applications out for large principal jobs in Illinois and Wisconsin. In West Liberty, I received an interview and did pretty well, according to the secretary of the Board. However, I didn't get the job. I remember feeling pretty disappointed about not being chosen, but it was the right decision by the West Liberty School Board. They hired an experienced superintendent better qualified to handle the current challenges confronting the school district.

I remember the Board president coming by my office, hoping to console me after hearing I was upset about being passed over. Heck, he didn't owe me any explanation. I do remember before he left, saying to me; "Jim, someday you are going to be one helluva superintendent for some school district."

In the coming weeks, I had three principal interviews in large schools, two in Illinois and one in Beloit, Wisconsin. As it turned out, not getting the West Liberty superintendent job was really a lucky break for me. In late July, I was appointed principal of Beloit Memorial High School in Wisconsin, one of the largest high schools in the state of Wisconsin. My dream came true, I was now the principal of a large high school.

A lesson I learned in the summer of 1986, which would repeat itself again later in my career, was that some jobs you don't get are a blessing in disguise. Keep the Faith! God is good!

Summary, Comments, and Takeaways from this Chapter

- Lost Nation: Learn to adapt to the surroundings you find yourself in.

- Leaders must use prudent judgement in making good decisions, which will not always be well received.

- Bob Steele, Del Jeneary, Mrs. B, Greg Guinn: It's the people you meet and the books you read that help you grow and meet your personal potential.

- Dirty Dilemmas: Sometimes in leadership, we have to find compromise: better to take that half a loaf of bread today, and live to fight another day tomorrow to get the other half.

- Until you are a victim of bias or discrimination yourself, you may never grasp the indignity and degradation of such acts.

Chapter 7

The Beloit Years (1986-1999)

In our last year in West Liberty, in the spring of 1986, Therese and I would sometimes joke that the next town we would live in would have a stoplight. Well, in mid-July, I was hired to become principal of Beloit Memorial High School (BMHS) in Beloit, Wisconsin, one of the largest high schools in the state. So, we definitely made the jump, there were plenty of stoplights. Beloit, Wisconsin, was a city of approximately thirty-five thousand citizens and very diverse with an urban flavor. My disappointment of not being selected superintendent in West Liberty vanished. When one door closes, another opens. Being appointed principal of Beloit Memorial was a dream come true!

Moving is never easy. My wife Therese was left to pack things up in West Liberty as I had to report and begin work at BMHS right away in mid-July, renting a room in a family's home. Janesville, a neighboring school district, had a one-year Spanish opening and hired Therese. That was a lucky break for us, as we struggled to sell our West Liberty home. We had two mortgages to pay off after buying our home in Beloit. While my salary had jumped from thirty-five thousand to fifty thousand in taking the Beloit job, we really needed Therese's income to handle the mortgages until our house finally sold in West Liberty a year later, where we took a loss.

Moving from a high school of four hundred students to a school that eventually would have twenty-two hundred students was quite a jump. Interestingly, I had interviewed in DeKalb, Illinois a couple of weeks before getting the BMHS job. I was told by the committee chair that the team that interviewed me was very impressed, however, the Board just could not see how a candidate could jump from a high school of four-hundred to a school of twelve-hundred. Well, I was happy the Beloit superintendent and Board of Education thought it could be done.

Admittedly, those first weeks were pretty overwhelming. I did have a week to work with the retiring principal, but I had no idea of how many tasks he left undone. Teachers were bitter over an arbitration case that gave them an extra supervisory duty, losing prep time (known as the sixth assignment on a seven-period day). Rooms that were to be refreshed with new coats of paint or new furniture, were not addressed. However, the worst thing I was blindsided by was that on the first day of school, over two-hundred students arrived without a class schedule. It took working day and night with my assistant principals and counselors to finally get everyone registered in classes. A week after the official start of school, we finally had all students registered with schedules. I vowed that, come the end of the current school year, students would be pre-registered for the following year, and have a schedule in hand before they left for summer vacation.

I had three assistant principals. This would be the first time I ever worked with assistant principals in a building. Beloit had a class principal concept where each principal was assigned a class. Francis (Fran) Fruzen was the senior class principal who also ran summer school and was in charge of the maintenance staff. Prior to becoming an administrator, Fran had been an outstanding social studies teacher and in his early years did some coaching. However, one of his greatest accomplishments was when he became president of the powerful Wisconsin Education Association Council (WEAC) in 1974. This was during some of the most bare-knuckle, arduous negotiations in the history of Wisconsin public education.

I was thirty-three, still pretty young and naïve. Fran was in his late fifties. It was only after being appointed that I became aware that

Fran had been an internal candidate for the job. I often wondered if his past WEAC union activism cost him the appointment. I can't think of any other reason. Fran had a stellar reputation as a teacher and a long-time assistant principal. He was also admired and respected by the teachers and staff.

I share the above because there is a great lesson here. Fran could have been bitter. However, as those first months of the school year progressed, he could not have been more supportive of me. I am sure there were times when he picked up on my inexperience as a large high school principal, but he did everything conceivable to see that I would succeed. In time, my knowledge base increased as the first semester of the school year moved forward.

Fran and I had a lot in common. We were both Catholic and men of deep Faith. We both had a strong work ethic that motivated us to really be invested in our work. We were the Beloit Memorial Purple Knights, and that spirit was the underpinning of the high school. We both wanted students, faculty, staff, families, and Beloit citizens to have pride in our school and feel a sense of loyalty and belonging. We both shared the philosophy that academics and structure must come first, and co-curricular activities were very important in the holistic development of our youth.

Another great influence on me was Dr. JB Elzy, a black assistant principal who helped and guided me immensely during my years in Beloit. He started the Minority Excellence Organization that encouraged our black students to achieve academically and become actively involved in school activities. Most importantly, through his lens as a black man, he could see and sense things that I could often miss when working with people of color. I remember he once told me; *"Jim, you are an honest and decent man, but you will never see things through the eyes of a black person."* To this day, I appreciated that advice JB gave me so long ago. I believe it helped me significantly in understanding cultural differences and perspectives.

Beloit Memorial already had a great sports tradition, winning conference and state titles in several sports. The theater department was second to none, putting on some amazing shows! Homecoming celebrations were huge, where the class competition for building the best homecoming float was really intense. The pep rallies were so much fun, and the people lined the streets as the homecoming parade proceeded downtown. A lucky break for me that first year was that the Purple Knight men's basketball team made it to the state tournament! I will never forget how the entire city of Beloit, got behind the team and our students as the school spirit flowed. People everywhere in Beloit were wearing Purple Knight shirts.

One of the best things about coming to Beloit was the professional development I received. The Effective Schools research, based on five strong correlates of sound school leadership, was some of the best training I ever received. There were other professional development opportunities, including teacher observation and evaluation, and school safety, including intruder training. Beloit was far ahead on safety training, long before Columbine. We were also one of the first to have a police-liaison officer (PLO) on campus. The PLO's we hired had a great rapport with our students.

A wonderful experience for me was working with department chairs. At Beloit Memorial, there were so many gifted teachers, it was the best teaching I would ever witness. I credit the department chairs for the pride they had in their departments and the high expectations they had for department members to be truly professional educators who prepared well and were student-focused. I remember when we would hire a new teacher, they were right away mentored by the department chair and embraced by department members. Veteran teachers willingly offered to share materials and resources to help in the induction of a new teacher. That was the first time I had witnessed that kind of collaborative teamwork.

Delegating and distributing leadership was a learning curve I had to adjust to. A principal cannot do it alone, and I still had a little of that small school principal mentality, despite the rapid growth I was making in my first year in Beloit. I would get much better at delegating in later years, especially when it came to working with department chairs, the guidance department, and the secretarial staff. I also got better working with committee structures. One committee particularly, was the multi-cultural committee that would become one of the most influential committees in the school.

Just before Christmas, my first year, I stopped by Fran's office just before calling it a day, about 6 PM. Everybody else was gone, and Fran and I were always the last people to leave. We would often have a conversation mulling over the day or the week. That night, just as I was ready to leave and say good night to Fran, he stopped me and said; *"Jim, this is a big operation, and you are doing a really good job!"* Fran was not one to throw around compliments unless he meant them genuinely. I thanked him for all his support, but his comment really put a hop in my step. One of my takeaways from that night was that affirmation is a powerful thing, never pass up a chance to credit your people for their great efforts. Fran modeled that for me.

After my first year, I was accepted nicely by the faculty, staff, and community. They noticed I was always visible, not one to hang around my office, I was out and around the entire school, especially during passing times, and had the same expectations of my three assistant principals. Discipline, communication, organization were all tightened up, and the faculty and staff really appreciated my efforts. I had earned their trust, and they knew I had their backs if their motives and methods were well intended. That is huge for a principal.

I was present at all co-curricular events, sports, musicals, plays, concerts, and JROTC events. I also joined the Rotary club, and made it a point to get out in the community, the coffee shops, and meet people, especially in the business community.

After our second year in Beloit, Therese was hired by Beloit Catholic High School. She would teach Spanish there for two years prior to being hired by the Beloit school district to teach at Aldrich Middle School, where she would teach for many years with a close-knit faculty who became some of her dearest friends.

Portrait in Purple Knight sweater – my last year in Beloit 1997.

The highlight for our family in our third year in Beloit was the birth of our son, Michael. Megan was now ten and in fourth grade. We were overjoyed to now have our second child. Beloit was a great place to raise our children, there was plenty for them to do with the parks and summer programs, the YMCA, which offered a nice venue for family activities and services. We also had some really nice neighbors, and as Megan and Mike grew up, there were friends in the neighborhood they could play with. There was a creek (Turtle Creek) behind our massive back yard where Megan and her girlfriends would often tube and float down the creek on hot summer days.

The city of Beloit and our school district had many of the same issues you find in urban cities. We had a high level of poverty in our community. Demographically, we were approximately sixty-five percent white, thirty-five percent black, with a smaller proportion of Asian, Latinx, and Native American families. Like in most communities, the Latinx population today has increased exponentially in Beloit.

I always thought our diversity was a gift, a bonus curriculum that students, upon graduating from Beloit Memorial, including my children, could go anywhere and adapt and flourish because they were exposed to diversity every day. Outside of Beloit, Milwaukee, Racine, and later on Madison were the only other cities that were demographically diverse. That, however, has changed with the large influx of Latinx families moving into the state. Now, almost every school district has an English Language Learning (ELL) program to meet the needs of non-native speakers.

We worked hard on cultural sensitivity and cultural competence long before DEI came to being. One of the greatest joys I had was working with a multi-cultural committee where we focused on highlighting the gifts and talents of all races and ethnicities. This committee was spawned by an incident where a leaflet was passed around the school with racist overtones, resulting in a rise of racial tension that took a couple of weeks to bring about some sense of healing. After this incident we met as a multi-cultural committee coming up with ideas on how everyone in the learning community would feel respected and valued in our learning community.

One of the strategies coming out of the multi-cultural committee was to organize and host a Worldfest day. This would be a festival where we celebrated all the different cultures represented in our community. Every member of the multi-cultural committee had a delegated task that might include bringing in ethnic food, or entertainers, music, art, and exhibits that were displayed in our huge field house. So many community people and businesses enthusiastically became involved in Worldfest. The highlight was an assembly where we had some wonderful music, dancing, inspiring talks, and videos that really got the student body involved and united in understanding that our diversity was indeed our strength.

BMHS was busting at the seams. We did not have enough classrooms, and we converted janitor closets and even bathrooms to make small learning areas and offices. We had some teachers who were on cart's moving from one classroom to another because we could not find a dedicated classroom for each full-time teacher. Bottom line, we needed to expand the school and add many more classrooms.

Simultaneously with our space shortage, there were discussions going on regarding grade level restructuring. BMHS included grades 10 through 12. The junior high included grades 7 through 9. Many ninth-grade students were matriculating to BMHS credit deficient, oblivious to the fact that their ninth-grade transcript grades counted toward graduation credits.

In these discussions, due to my past experience in West Liberty and Newman, I believed the ninth graders belonged in the high school building. Those advocating for a middle school concept argued that the junior high concept should give way to grades 6 through 8. A more affective approach with smaller house concepts would bolster academic achievement and was a holistically better approach for students ten to fourteen years old.

For this transition to happen, BMHS would need to under-go a massive expansion and remodeling to accommodate a shift of five-hundred ninth graders to the high school. In one of the most exciting experiences of my life, we embarked on convincing the citizens of Beloit to pass a referendum for 26.5 million dollars to expand BMHS. We spent months working with architects. In the winter and early spring of 1992, we were out almost every night holding meetings and public engagements, trying to convince the business community and citizens we needed to expand BMHS to make room for the ninth grade. The expansion would enlarge BMHS from two-hundred and twenty thousand square feet to four-hundred and sixty-thousand square feet, doubling the size of the facility.

May 14, 1992, will always remain one of the greatest days of my life. In a special election, the citizens of Beloit approved overwhelmingly a twenty-six-million-dollar referendum to move forward with the expansion. I remember there was a gathering in the district board room. When the final tallies came in we jumped for joy that it passed. Now the real work would begin with a two-year construction program. Somehow we survived the hammering and drilling and in the fall of 1995 the freshman class was welcomed to BMHS with the four-year enrollment now soaring to twenty-two hundred students. The finished product was magnificent. We now had adequate space and a high school facility that was modern and would serve the community well into the next century.

Now that the space issue was addressed, we needed to bolster academic achievement. While we had tremendous programs, including AP and vocational programming, and a wonderful arts program, we needed to do some things structurally in the way we delivered our curriculum so more of our students would find a pathway to success. Upon visiting Champlin Park, Minnesota, a couple of years earlier to get ideas on what a recently built new high school should look like, we also discovered they had a four-block schedule. Most high schools operate on six, seven, or eight period schedules spanning from 40 to 55 minutes per period. This block schedule was for 90 minutes, and students only took four classes a day.

At Beloit Memorial, we had a seven-period day. Most student took five or six subjects. What bothered me was that if a student fell behind in credits, we often loaded them up with seven classes to catch them up. What would happen was that they would fail miserably, even falling further behind in their attainment of credits.

It also occurred to me that what Champlin Park was doing made sense. Students who would go on to colleges and universities rarely had a class load of more than four courses a semester. If that was suffice for our most successful learners, why were we overloading our struggling high school learners with seven courses or eight (if on an eight-period day)?

We began a study as a faculty. This would prove to be one of the great leadership lessons I would ever learn when it came to bringing about major change in an organization. How does a leader get BUY-IN for a new initiative change?

We first studied our data. There was little disagreement that we had too many students receiving failing grades. We then took some field trips to schools that had four-block schedules, including Brentwood High School near St. Louis. We then made another trip to Champlin Park, Minnesota, where, on an off day, we took a busload of teachers and several student leaders from the junior and senior classes. Champlin Park and Brentwood administrators, faculty, and staff could not have been more helpful and honest it in sharing the pros and some cons of the four-block. We wanted an honest appraisal of this schedule. The overwhelming sentiment at both schools was very favorable in terms of their experience. Grades and graduation rates had improved. Borrowing ideas and concepts from other schools and organizations is a good practice. We often isolate ourselves. Seeing what other schools or organizations are doing is a good way to accelerate change when you are stuck.

Upon reflection, I didn't realize we were really following the 8-steps for change that Dr. John Kotter espoused, which included creating a sense of urgency, building a coalition of support, and creating a vision. After the trips to Brentwood and Champlin Park, I now had an army of supporters who could help me sell the vision to the rest of the faculty.

It took almost a year to get significant buy-in from the faculty, but taking the time to gain consensus was well worth it. I didn't want this to be a top-down standoff with the union. Moreover, I wanted the teachers to eventually embrace the idea. After much study, continued data collection, and discussion often led by teacher leaders who were now behind the four-block, it was agreed that if eighty-percent of the faculty would vote in favor of the new schedule, we would implement it the following year. The final vote that October was almost ninety-percent in favor. One of the provisos of the vote was that after three-semesters we would have another vote to determine whether the four block should be continued. Again, the threshold was to be an eighty percent approval vote. It once again passed by almost a ninety percent margin.

Students and parents were almost unanimously in favor of the schedule as well. They had been involved in presentations and engagements prior to the change. What I learned from this process was that it was not the schedule itself, but the communication and the decision-making process that was so important in attaining the buy-in. After this experience, I knew for the rest of my career never to rush a decision that didn't need to be made prematurely. Seek the buy-in first.

Things continued to go very well for me in my years at BMHS. We would become an exemplary high school in the state, and soon were gaining national recognition as over two hundred schools from all over the country came to observe our four-block and hear our presentation. With a team of teachers, we often presented at state association conferences. We also hit the road showcasing our four-block and our amazing consensus decision-making process in several school districts in Wisconsin and Illinois. It was a great feeling to become a renowned high school. It was also a shot in the arm for the community of Beloit that had long suffered from a negative reputation.

As year eleven was coming to a close and my daughter Megan was ready to graduate from BMHS, I began thinking about earning my doctoral degree. Before leaving West Liberty, I was well on my way with over sixty hours beyond the Masters Degree. I had some unfinished business in my desire to earn my doctoral degree.

In earlier chapters, I expressed my disdain for standardized and timed exams. I never performed well on them. When I moved to Wisconsin, I tried to gain acceptance into their Educational Leadership program at the University of Wisconsin, Madison. My Graduate Record Exams scores were not high enough, and unlike Iowa, Wisconsin (UW) would not accept me. As the years went on, I would have BMHS faculty members taking admin courses at UW, and they would often ask me to be a guest speaker. I often gave presentations on being the principal of an urban and diverse high school, or on bringing about change with our four-block experience.

One day after a UW presentation, the professor, who was also the chair of the Ed. Admin department said to me; *"you should really get into our program and earn your doctorate."* He knew me pretty well from previous presentations to his class. I told him I tried, but my test scores, while good enough for Iowa, were not good enough for UW-

Madison. My tone was a bit belligerent, because by this time, I knew I was a good principal, and so did he! He said, *"let me get back to you."* A couple of weeks later, he called me and said; *"we can accept you as a guest student and then see how you do. If you do well, I will advocate for you to be admitted to our program."* I said; *"That would be fine, give me the toughest son of bitch professor you have in the department and I will prove I belong at UW!"*

True to his word, he did assign me to a very demanding professor. The course was Politics of Education, right up my alley after eleven years in Beloit. I did well, and both the department chair and the Politics professor lobbied for my acceptance, waiving the GRE. I was admitted to the doctoral program at UW-Madison.

The principalship of Beloit Memorial deserved one-hundred percent dedication. I knew I had to be all in on my doctoral studies to complete them within two years, a goal Therese and I had discussed. I announced in May my resignation as principal of Beloit Memorial effective June 30, 1997. It had been a magical eleven-year run. The faculty at my last meeting gave me a generous gift with many tributes, along with a roasting. Later, there was a community celebration held in my honor. A scholarship in my name was established. For the next two-years, I was off to UW to earn my doctorate degree by the spring of 1999.

Therese continued to teach at Aldrich as I began my doctoral studies for the next two years. She would pick up any extra-duty jobs she could, including covering periods for absent teachers to coaching the bowling team. Fiscally, we were very frugal, living now off her income, mostly with the exception of some four-block consulting jobs I contracted, along with some part-time administrative work I did at Madison LaFollette High School, where I worked with the senior class. LaFollette had just implemented the four-block schedule, so I was helping them with that as well.

During my eleven years in Beloit, there were six permanent or interim superintendents. Frankly, there were only two that I really respected, and one got fired due mostly to board and union politics. The others seemed to be only using Beloit as a stepping stone, not really invested in staying long in the community. So, as I began my doctoral studies, I was not really sure I wanted to become a superintendent.

In my doctoral dissertation research, I focused on Superintendents in the state of Wisconsin. I was interested in finding out what superintendents were like outside of Beloit. I wanted to find out what they valued in their decision-making. My findings indicated that superintendents considered four dimensions in their decision making: the ethical, legal, financial, and political considerations in arriving at decisions.

Overwhelmingly, I found that most superintendents were indeed motivated to be ethical in their decision-making and their approach to their jobs. While acknowledging they did need to have some political awareness and savvy, they would not abandon their own personal values and sense of ethics for political gain. This was somewhat surprising to me because I rarely observed this in Beloit.

The dissertation process and my studies at UW Madison persuaded me to seriously consider the superintendency just at a time when the Beloit superintendent job came open. The superintendent left for a bigger urban job in Ohio. I was about eight months away from completing my doctoral requirements.

The assistant superintendent for business was named interim superintendent, and a nation-wide search commenced. I decided I would apply, but first asked the interim superintendent, who had been a good colleague of mine, if he would be willing to stay on as interim superintendent until I was conferred my degree on May 14, 1999, still several months away. He graciously told me he would be happy to do that for me!

I applied for the position, sharing with the Board that I would pledge to serve no less than ten years, while understanding fully I would be working at the pleasure of the Board. Instability with superintendents coming and going had hurt the district for many years. I promised to be truly invested in the district and the community, as I had been as principal of BMHS, where I had gained great respect from families and the business community.

The only downside to my candidacy was lacking superintendent experience. Another consideration for the Board was whether to wait for me to finish my doctorate, still several months away, but in capable hands of the interim superintendent. I learned later in a 4-3 vote in closed session, the Board decided not to interview me despite an editorial in the *Beloit Daily News* encouraging the Board to put me on the short list for an interview. The bottom line was the Board did not want to wait, and felt safer hiring a candidate with experience, who, like previous superintendents, would leave after a short tenure.

I loved Beloit, and I was devastated to not even get a shot at interviewing for the job. I think for the first time in my life, I was truly depressed. I had given my heart and soul to that district as principal of BMHS for eleven years. To this day, I feel I could have made a great difference in Beloit in advancing the school district and the community. I was eager to work with community leaders and citizens to truly make our school district and community a great place to live and raise a family.

It's funny how you revert back to what has been instilled in you throughout your life. As sad as I was to be out of the running for the Beloit superintendency, I still had work to do in completing my doctoral studies and defending my dissertation in March of 1999. Those lessons learned from Coach Pauls and Coach Hoppenstedt of maintaining self-discipline and grit did not allow me to wallow in my sorrows for very long.

I also thought of my mom and dad and how they coped with bad news and moved on from it. The inspiring lessons I had learned from Fathers McClean and Gehling also kicked in, reminding me of the power of prayer and to lean into my faith when facing any hardship. I even thought of Fran and wondered now if I had some idea of the hurt and disappointment he went through when he was passed over in favor of me in becoming principal of BMHS. But it was from Therese that I drew my greatest inspiration. She knew how bad I wanted this job, we both loved Beloit. She saw first-hand the sacrifices we made during my eleven years at BMHS. She picked up my spirits, assuring me something better was going to come our way.

Therese proved to be prophetic. The school district of Fort Atkinson, about thirty miles north of Beloit, posted an opening for a superintendent. I applied for the position and received two interviews. Ironically, on St. Patrick's day, March 17[th,] 1999, I was offered the appointment, which I happily accepted. The timing was now right, my doctoral degree would be conferred on May 14[th,] and my first day on the job was to be July 1, 1999. Suddenly, my time at UW was over after two intense years, as was my time in Beloit. We would now be moving into the community of Fort Atkinson to start the next chapter in our lives. Megan was finishing up at UW, and Mike would be moving on to fifth grade in a new community.

Summary Comments, and leadership takeaways from this Chapter:

- Some of the jobs you don't get turn out to be a blessing; when one door closes, another often opens.
- Fran Fruzen: handle disappointment with grace and never miss an opportunity to affirm the good efforts of others.
- When initiating change, take the time to collaborate and gain buy-in.

- In leadership, you cannot do it alone, delegate to others in helping you achieve a desired outcome.
- Standardized exams used as an exclusionary tool have resulted in missed opportunities for some potentially great leaders.
- Keep the Faith, even in your darkest hour, lean into prayer, it brings you to a better place.

Chapter 8

The Superintendency Fort Atkinson, WI 1999-2013

March 1999 was a whirlwind time in our lives. I defended my dissertation in early March. Later in the month, two school districts interviewed me for their superintendent vacancies. The Milton and Fort Atkinson school districts bordered each other and had strikingly similar timelines for hiring their next superintendent.

I was pretty committed to accepting the first offer that came my way if the compensation package met our expectations. We were barely getting by, mostly on Therese's salary for the previous two years while I was working on my degree. The only scary thing about Milton was that their previous superintendent had also served as the business director. While there were overtures that they might hire a business director, there were no promises. That made me a bit uncomfortable. Sure, I knew how to manage a large high school budget, but a district budget, that was a whole other ballgame. Understanding taxation, forecasting revenue sources, expenditures, state aid, federal grants, and so many other responsibilities that business directors oversee, seemed a bit daunting. Luckily the Fort Atkinson offer came first, and I accepted, and would you believe the offer came on St. Patrick's Day, March 17th? How lucky could an Irishman get!

Conversely, Fort Atkinson had a brilliant Director of Business. I am pretty convinced that his expertise per fiscal matters was why the Board took a chance on selecting me, without any superintendent or central office experience, rather than two other finalists who were superintendents.

A favorite picture of Therese and me in Fort Atkinson 2000.

While my two-years of doctoral studies were exciting, they were also very stressful for Therese and me. It was also a sad time. My father was battling cancer and was eventually placed in Hospice care. I would drive in from Wisconsin to see him in his last months, and his positive attitude always amazed me. One day, I walked in and he was reading the Chicago Tribune. I asked him how he was doing. Smiling, he said, *"great, I just finished reading the obituaries and I am still here!"* Right up to the end, he was always upbeat and interested in knowing how my studies and dissertation were going. He passed away on September 18, 1998.

We were ready for some joy and celebrating following the commencement ceremony on May 14, 1999, when my degree was conferred. We invited over a hundred family members and friends from Beloit to celebrate in a big party we had at the Hilton Hotel in Madison. I had earned some extra money doing some four-block consulting presentations, so I wanted to splurge! In addition, I purchased a larger diamond for Therese's wedding ring in an expression of my love and appreciation for her. She was a real trooper, making many sacrifices so I could achieve my dream. My new job in Fort Atkinson (Fort) would begin officially on July 1, we had a month to decompress and now find a new home.

Loved those cross-country meets. Here with my Fort Blackhawks

Unlike our previous move from Iowa, this time our home in Beloit sold fairly quickly and for a good price. This gave us an opportunity to make an offer on a nice home in our new community.

By mid-July, after living in a hotel for two weeks, we moved into our new house. Therese would continue teaching Spanish in Beloit, but now had a forty-five-minute commute. A year later, she would be hired by the neighboring Jefferson School District to teach high school Spanish. It was a trade-off in that it was only a ten-minute commute to Jefferson, but she took a hit on her salary.

Graduation picture with My Son Mike 2007

The Fort Board of Education (BOE) and Administration had been engaging in strategic planning. The core of the planning committee was made up of teachers, principals, BOE members, staff, parents, citizens, and business leaders-a very good cross-section of stakeholders. In this revisioning effort, the committee was charged with developing a district mission, vision, philosophy, and short and long-term goals. Even though I was not scheduled to start in my new role before July 1st, I was invited in to listen as the five-year strategic plan was finalized, and ready to present to the BOE for final approval.

Fort Atkinson graduation–June 2008

I really liked the mission statement: *"The School District of Fort Atkinson is committed to providing programs and services so that all students will have the opportunity to realize their academic and personal potential!* This mission really aligned with everything I have ever believed in throughout my career. There were also three major goals that were to be achieved before this five-year plan expired:

1. Provide early interventions for our learners.
2. Relieve crowding in elementary buildings, including the re-purposing of the Luther building (formerly a middle school, now vacant except for a section housing the central office).
3. Restore trust in the district.

Picture with Therese at our lake house 2013

The strategic plan, while serving as a road map for the district and me as the new superintendent, was surely going to be helpful as I began my duties, but it hardly gave me what I really needed to know about the culture of the district. In an early retreat with BOE members after about a month on the job, I found out that the strategic plan, which also called for a more democratic approach to district governance, was not really embraced by a couple of Board members, who were reluctant to buy-into a more collaborative governance style. This surprised me a little, given the unanimous approval of the plan, a month earlier.

Whether you are coming in as a new principal or superintendent, there are *some key questions* you want to pose to stakeholders as you begin in a new school or district. These questions will give you an early assessment of the present culture, providing you with insight as you begin your principalship or superintendency.

Below are the five questions I sent out to all certified and uncertified staff through a SurveyMonkey that was anonymous, but I was surprised by how many willingly shared their names. In addition to the questions below, I included a checklist for respondents indicating their roles (such as teacher, principal, assistant principal, guidance, librarian (media specialist, IT, aide, custodian, secretary etc.).

The five Key questions:

Question 1: What are the strengths of the district?

Question 2: What might be areas that need some attention or improvement?

Question 3: If you had a problem, personal or professional, who might you confide in at your school (or in the district)?

Question 4: Who are parents, community members, or business leaders who have been strong supporters of our schools?

Question 5: In looking forward to working with you, is there anything else you would like to share with me at this time?

Question 1, immediately informed me of the strengths, rituals, and traditions that were a sense of pride in the Fort Atkinson School District. This was very important. A mistake many leaders make is to come in with their own agenda while ignoring the cultural richness that may already exist and should be embraced. I found out right away the rituals and traditions that should be continued under my leadership.

Question 2, yielded a tremendous amount of information regarding some things that were not going well. Note how I phrased the question! The word *weaknesses* was not used for fear of offending however, weaknesses and discontent feelings are exactly what people shared with me, and many were recurring comments about mistrust with the central administration and some building leadership.

Question 3, immediately informed me who were the influential leaders in the schools and the district, and where the power resided. As a superintendent you learn that it is difficult to succeed if you try to do the job alone. You have to be willing to delegate. In building a distributive leadership approach, which enhances the culture, this question informed me of the informal leaders who were trusted by others. These people can help you build relational trust. Invariably, I saw the same names popping up.

One might assume that if faculty and staff had a professional problem, they might confide in either the principal or the union rep in their building. While this is sometimes the case, very often others on the staff are sought out. These are the informal leaders. There is a difference between *power and authority*. The title may give you authority, but the power and influence you earn! I found out who these trusted and valued informal leaders were even before I formally met them.

Question 4, gave me knowledge of parents, community members, and business people who were supportive of the schools and understood the importance of the district in the community. My next step was to reach out to these parents and community leaders, and ask them to respond to questions 1, 2, 4, and 5.

Parents and community members added names that faculty and staff did not identify. When I contrasted the internal and external responses, I found some common ground, some differences, and a few surprises per how employees and external stakeholders viewed the district.

Question 5, rendered me a plethora of opinions and thoughts not covered in the previous four questions. The key wording in this question was- *In looking forward to* ***working with you*** *as your new* *superintendent,* I wanted to set a collaborative tone! *Together,* we can move Fort Atkinson forward.

This survey really gave me some insight just six weeks into my new job. Many of the respondents added a thank you to me for reaching out and taking an interest in what they had to say. Several noted that they were looking forward to meeting me. While there were some positives, overall, I learned the morale was pretty low with a lot of distrust. It was July, and teacher contract negotiations were not going well, and I really wanted to get a contract settled before the start of the new school year. Furthermore, there was a bitter insurance arbitration grievance that was really getting ugly. Just like when I arrived in Beloit, the learning community in Fort, seemed to be in a rough place.

The Director of Business had actually negotiated a brilliant health insurance plan where if claims did not reach a certain level of the renewal contract, the district would be rebated back the difference. Sure enough, the insurance company had to rebate money back to the district. The teacher union grieved that, due to the monthly premiums being paid they were entitled to some of the insurance rebate money (as did administrators in the district).

This insurance rebate issue was far more complex than what I explained above. I sat through one arbitration hearing. Before leaving the hearing room, the arbitrator indicated he would rule on the case within sixty-days. I knew I didn't want to wait for his decision. If the arbitrator ruled in favor of the BOE and the stance of the Director of Business, I would never gain the trust of this faculty and staff, and this was not the way to start a superintendency. I convinced the BOE to acknowledge the Union grievance so we could move on and get out from under this cloud. It did not take much persuading, they, too, were exhausted and wanted an end to this grievance. The Arbitrator was informed that the grievance had been settled, and shortly after, teachers and administrators received rebate reimbursement checks.

My decision was a tough blow for the Director of Business, who had spent hours on end preparing for the arbitration. I deeply respected him for the diligence and actual genius he often displayed in his role. However, this had turned into a power struggle. Sometimes you may win the battle but lose the war. This decision went a long way in regaining the trust of the faculty and staff. This, along with settling the contract just before the school year began, were the first steps in building relational trust in the district. I was off to a pretty good start.

In Fort Atkinson, at the beginning of the school year a Convocation is held. The highlight of the event is to honor a teacher who had demonstrated excellence with the Wildermuth Award, named after an educator who tragically died in a motorcycle accident. This was a very coveted award, and a great honor for the recipient. At that event, the superintendent also delivers a speech welcoming the staff back for another school year, along with sharing some of the goals for the year. The cabinet thought I should highlight the newly approved Strategic Plan.

This was my first Convocation speech and the only time you were really in front of the entire faculty and staff. There is an expression that you never get a second chance to make a first impression. As I approached the podium, there was dead silence. I had the feeling that, as the new superintendent, many wondered; *what do we have here?* I decided this was not the day to talk about the new strategic plan, goals, curriculum, or new policies. I wanted to speak from the heart in genuinely sharing with all assembled, how honored I was to be their superintendent, and how much I was looking forward to working with them. I made an appeal to everyone in the auditorium, humbly acknowledging that I could not do this job alone, and as valued members of this learning community, I would need their help. I closed my comments stating; *"Together let's make Fort Atkinson a beacon school district in this state, where there is a sense of caring and belonging!"*

My comments were well received, and as I walked off the stage, I was surprised to see the standing ovation. I was starting to make some connections, so important to reaching that goal of district trust. It had to start with trust in me.

One of my first important jobs was to hire a principal at one of the elementary schools. I worked with the faculty and staff of that elementary, and we developed the profile of the principal candidate we hoped to attract. Three weeks later, by the second week of August, we had our new principal, who would go on to do a really nice job.

This was also my first experience working with a central office cabinet team and then a full-fledged administrative team that included principals, assistant principals, and the cabinet. The full cabinet met every Tuesday morning, consisting of the Directors from Business, Curriculum, Pupil Services, Technology, and Building and Grounds. We generally met for two-hours planning for BOE agendas, reviewing strategic plan goals, and addressing issues that might arise so we could be pro-active. I would also meet daily for a quick calendar meeting with the directors of curriculum, business, and pupil services, also keeping an eye on hot issues.

The full Administrative team meetings were held once a month late in the day, limiting the time principals would need to be out of their buildings, usually running from 2 PM to 4:30 PM. The district had six schools-four elementary buildings (eventually, although when I started three), a middle school and a high school.

One of the important things I learned in leading the formal cabinet and administrative meetings was to have an organized agenda and packet ready for these meetings. I also made sure my assistant recorded minutes so that I could always look back and see if we followed through on planning and decisions.

Our BOE meeting was held on the third Thursday of each month. We only held one meeting a month unless there was a need for a special BOE meeting. We did have three sub-committees for Policy, Curriculum, and Finance, where two BOE members would serve on each of these committees as appointed by the BOE president.

Typically, in preparing for a Board meeting, I would meet with the president and sometimes another BOE member on the Friday before our monthly meeting in going over the BOE agenda. In Fort, we had five board members. This was also a time for me to brief the president and BOE members on any other developments. Upon finalizing the agenda, we would include a packet with administrative notes regarding each item on the agenda. Early the following week, I would meet in pairs with the rest of the members prior to my cabinet meeting on Tuesday morning of Board meeting week. I made sure that at these monthly briefings, I rotated members so the five would always be interacting with different BOE members.

By Tuesday morning, I would have briefed all BOE members. I could now inform the cabinet members of any questions or concerns BOE members would want addressed at the Thursday BOE meeting. I had an understanding with the BOE that they would never be surprised at the Board table, and I would expect the same from them, so the briefings prepared both of us.

Systems are important in leadership, especially communication systems. Each Friday, I would send notes to the BOE members, keeping them up to speed on developments -often celebrations and good news, or legislative issues coming down the pike that might result in policy changes. I would also send out monthly faculty and family newsletters (From the Superintendent's Desk), often kick-starting them with a quote at the beginning, keeping everyone in the learning community informed. I especially enjoyed highlighting celebrations, accomplishments, and good news, along with important events coming up. I wanted to be not only the superintendent but the number one cheerleader in boosting the support and spirit for our school district. However, I also understood the need to convey information regarding serious issues with candidness and honesty. I often received nice comments in passing or nice emails and notes for sharing my thoughts and news.

The Daily Jefferson County Union was a newspaper published daily, Monday through Friday, that covered all the local news. It covered our BOE meetings, sporting events, concerts, and all school and district activities. Social media, Facebook pages, and websites were just coming onto the scene. The Daily Union had a wide readership following in Fort Atkinson and our county. I asked if I could write a column each month entitled *KEEPING YOU INFORMED* The editor and publisher welcomed my column, and now I had another way to reach out to the community on information and developments impacting our district.

I always felt it was important to develop a good working relationship with the local press, after an unpleasant experience I once had in West Liberty. We also had a radio station where I was invited on many occasions to share news with the listeners, especially when we were hoping to pass referendums, which later in my tenure became a consuming part of the job.

Picture stories are some of the best ways to promote success. Before every BOE meeting, the Daily Union beat reporter would take pictures, mostly of students and staff who had accomplished great things. Maybe national merit winners, Rotary teachers of the month, award winners in sports, music, forensics, or any accomplishments worthy of recognition from the BOE. There is so much good news that often goes unrecognized in a school district. Since *No Child Left Behind,* it seemed the ultimate measure of a learning community was how its students performed on standardized exams. I made a vow to myself that these exams, just a small snapshot of what goes on in a school district, were not going to hijack the great story we had to share! I never wanted to miss an opportunity to promote our successes. One other benefit of the picture stories was that no matter how tough a BOE meeting might be with some controversial issues, I knew that in the Friday afternoon paper, there would be some good news picture stories taking up plenty of square inches of print!

Almost daily, there would be a pictures of school activities. It might be students who performed well on AP Exams, at anFBLA conference, or at an Art show. I would clip these pictures out, and in a card entitled, *You are in the News,-* send these to the kids. They loved them, and upon graduation, I often saw them in their portfolios that they had to present as a graduation requirement. Parents noticed these notes as well—there is an old saying, *"if you want to win the hearts of parents it is through the kid."* The newspaper also reported on local businesses and their success or people in their organizations being promoted. I sent clips and cards to them as well.

In my second year as superintendent in April of 2001, tragedy befell our community. Four students coming home from a Young Republicans youth conference were tragically killed in a car accident where they collided with a semi-truck at an intersection of two country roads on a Friday night. At approximately 10 PM, I received a call from the Sherriff's office requesting the use of our high school office so they could meet with the parents to inform them of the tragedy, and sadly, to identify the bodies of their children. I had never witnessed such grief in my life. Therese accompanied me to the high school, holding one of the mothers in her arms.

I will always be grateful for the support I received from my administrative team and especially Joe Overturf, our director of pupil services, who led the effort in providing counseling for so many grieving students and adults. The following day (Saturday and extending into Sunday), we opened the school for students and families to come and grieve.

We had to cancel all sporting events scheduled for that Saturday, getting great support and assistance from the athletic director and the coaches. The high school principal had an emergency meeting with his faculty and staff that Sunday, in making preparations on how to proceed on Monday when grieving students would be returning to school. Food was provided by local businesses. Several ministers, faculty, and parents were present to console students. We had sheets of poster paper where the students with sharpies would write their condolence messages to their lost friends. These were posted all over the walls of our large cafeteria/commons area. It seemed cathartic for them to get out their feelings of loss. In the days to follow, there were four separate visitations and funerals. I attended all of them and wrote a column in the paper expressing sorrow and support for the families of these loved ones.

How were we going to get passed this horrific tragedy? It's amazing how your faith, and in my case, my Catholicism, seemed to kick into a higher gear. It also seemed helpful that I grew up in a family so connected to the funeral business that almost innately I understood many of the things that would need to done in the upcoming days. I found myself praying, like I had never prayed before for the families of these children. I prayed that, as the leader of this school district, please God give me the strength to make all the right decisions in getting us past the despair and anguish that now gripped our community. I also prayed that God would bless all of our students, faculty, and staff so deeply hurt by this loss. It wasn't just the students we had to care for who lost their friends, but teachers and staff as well, who had made close connections with these kids, they needed interventions as well.

You often hear of the separation of church and state when it comes to public schooling. This tragic event brought both institutions together. I will always be deeply indebted to three ministers in the community who took the lead in organizing a community service on Wednesday night following the accident. We had thousands of people from the community pack the gymnasium to support the grieving families. In a beautifully organized program by the ministers and our music department, there was a mix of musical tributes, and student testimonials celebrating the lives of each of the four students. The ministers delivered passages from scripture, along with comforting words, sensitively and lovingly delivered.

Hardly a day goes by that I don't think about this tragic occurrence, especially now, years later, when I see the parents. Oh, how I wished we could turn back the clock and undo what happened. In every cloud, it is often said, there is some silver lining. Not in this case. However, I do believe this tragedy united our community in bringing us closer together, and was a defining benchmark of my superintendency in efforts to bring healing and closure. I will always be thankful for the efforts of my administrative team, the faculty and staff, the ministers, and the community leaders who God sent my way during this most difficult time.

We were building relational trust in the school district and the community. To relieve overcrowding in the three existing elementary schools, after much study, we were able to renovate and re-purpose the Luther building into our fourth elementary school in the 2000-2001 school year. That same year, we started all-day kindergarten, thus resolving the Luther building utilization issue, and taking one more step forward in addressing early interventions with the implementation of all-day kindergarten.

I now chuckle a bit when I reflect on a rough public engagement that took place at one of our elementary buildings in our efforts to gain support for all day kindergarten. As I was leaving, a mother grabbed me by the cuff of my suit coat and said, *"Fitzpatrick, I suppose the next thing you will be pushing will be four-year-old kindergarten."* As I got out the door, I smiled to myself and thought YEP! In the Fall of 2008, we implemented 4-year-old kindergarten!

We still had a lot to do in the way of providing our youngest learners early interventions. We moved to all-day kindergarten, feeling instructionally these little children could handle it. Too often in the past, we put our resources into high school students who were at risk of not graduating. Often this was too late. Investing in early interventions for our youngest learners just seemed to make a lot of sense, especially if we could get them to break that code we call READING as early as possible.

By 2007, it was time to create a new strategic plan, the goals and outcomes of the initial strategic plan implemented in 1999 were now institutionalized. Our next five-year strategic plan to span from 2008 to 2013 would focus much more on curriculum realignment vertical and horizontal, new program adoptions in mathematics and science, and most importantly a robust literacy program. In addition, we wanted to explore green energy sources for cost savings and environmental reasons, there were a lot of incentives being offered.

We dedicated a great deal of time and energy in developing a strong literacy program. We started an intense Reading Recovery program for students in first and second grade who were struggling as beginning readers. Later, we adopted a Comprehensive Literacy Model. We also developed programming for dyslexic children. We wanted a wide variety of strategies to help our readers. Our Director of Curriculum and Instruction and our reading teachers and coaches really worked hard to make our reading program not only one of the best in the state, but nationally renowned as well! We also developed strong Multi-tiered systems of support (MTSS) at all grade levels in the elementary schools, to meet academic and social-emotional needs.

While we were focused on early interventions we did not want to abandon our at-risk older students. One of the best initiatives we implemented in the district was the Crossroads program for at-risk high school students. For some teens, the traditional large high school is just not a good fit. The Crossroads program was a small, intimate program with maybe ten students in the morning and ten in the afternoon for mostly seventeen-year-olds who were credit deficient. It was competency based versus the Carnegie unit way of earning credit. When they reached mastery of all the requirements, they could graduate. The students would receive instruction in the core subjects for half a day, and receive co-op work credit for jobs they were placed in.

During my tenure of fourteen years, I witnessed hundreds of at-risk students graduating who without Crossroads, would have dropped out of school with little hope for the future. Many have gone on to have successful careers and lives. The key was having a very gifted teacher who led the Crossroads program. The kids believed in him because of the balance of empathy, firmness, and structure he was able to deliver in a magnificent way.

We had some aging buildings without air conditioning. We wanted to expand our summer school programming and leave open the concept of year-round schooling, maybe someday in the future. After a great amount of study, including trips with BOE members to Cedar Rapids and Dubuque, Iowa, we saw first-hand how buildings seventy-years old, were renovated with geothermal heating and cooling systems. When Iowa officials shared with us the savings they incurred on energy bills and the payback for installation not exceeding ten years, the BOE became convinced we should go to the electorate for a referendum to convert four of our aging buildings to geothermal energy.

We had one other daunting issue facing public schools in Wisconsin. The legislature had established revenue limits per how much property tax a district could levy. The limits were initially temporary but were made permanent in the 1995-97 state biennial budget (1995 Act 27). The purpose of these revenue limits was to control property taxes by limiting the amount of revenue school districts could raise through state general aid and local property taxes. The revenue limits combined with declining pupil enrollment in most districts, including Fort Atkinson, resulted in budget shortfalls.

I was optimistic that our community engagements on geothermal systems and our need for voters to approve our request to exceed the revenue limits would pass. I thought surely people would understand that we could not jeopardize the programs and services we needed to serve our students. Boy, was I wrong! The referendum failed by a large margin.

This was the beginning of employing task forces in our community to help guide me and the BOE on critical decisions impacting local taxpayers. We invited a gifted facilitator to help us get ready for the following spring election in April, and another try to pass the referendum. However, first, she insisted we find out why we failed the previous October. Through a survey, we found out that taxpayers were uncomfortable with a *recurring* referendum, or as many referred to it as a "blank check" that would go on for perpetuity. From the survey, we did learn that there would be support for a *non-recurring* referendum for a period of 3-5 years, with the BOE and the administration coming back to the taxpayers if we needed more support.

These taskforce meetings were sometimes painful for me to sit through. There was a mix of pro-school district citizens along with conservative tax-payer watchdogs. One guy in particular, Bob Baxter (pseudonym), was really difficult. He was a retired lawyer who would try to dominate discussions, and was always critical of me and the administration claiming we would not need more money if we knew how to use our resources wisely. He definitely thought he was the smartest guy in the room. Even the skilled facilitator had a tough time shutting him down. While he was getting under my skin, I came to realize that nobody else on the taskforce including some of the more conservative members really paid much attention to anything he said.

The facilitator did her job, in getting the taskforce to reach a consensus on a *non-recurring* referendum that the BOE supported and in April 2006, the referendum passed. I was thrilled. We now had what we needed to install geothermal heating and cooling systems in four of our aging buildings, along with enough money for operations the next five years, in providing programs, services, and staffing needs until 2011 when we would have to come back to the citizens again with another non-recurring referendum.

Another key initiative in the new strategic plan was the adoption of a four-year old kindergarten program (4-K). Two-years earlier, the Wisconsin Department of Public Instruction (DPI) recommended possible models for schools to consider. Due to a lack of space in our buildings, we chose a model where we could partner with other Fort Atkinson community day care agencies.

Like school districts, these agencies were also often strapped for revenue streams, and a sixty/forty split in the revenues received for the 4K per pupil enrollment turned out to be a win-win fiscal proposition for the district and the day-cares! We required the agencies to implement the 4K curriculum we developed. The agencies were required to hire a licensed early child hood teacher (PreK through grade 2 license).

Many local churches offered day care and wanted to be partners with the district. They agreed to offer secular programming free of religious indoctrination, making sure crucifixes, icons, or paintings were removed from the 4K room. This was a requirement that had to be honored and would be audited by state officials who made site visits.

The 4K programs were half day programs but most agencies had wrap- around programming that was attractive to working parents, who could pick their children up after work. This was a critical program in providing early intervention. We were leveling the playing field for all children entering five-year old kindergarten, not just the ones whose parents could afford high quality day care.

In 1997 the legislature in Wisconsin under Act 27 adopted the Open Enrollment Law, which allowed a student to attend any public school district in the state. No longer was a student required to attend school in the district where the family resided. Initially this law had little impact. However, as the temporary revenue limits became permanent (as they are to this day), many financially strapped districts started to lose students to districts offering more desirable programming. Approximately seventy-percent of the per pupil cost followed the student to the new accepting district.

After the 2006 Fort Atkinson referendum passed allowing us to keep our programs ~~intact~~ intact with desirable class sizes we began to accept more open enrollment students into our district. We had a robust music, fine arts, practical arts, and sports program as well as all-day kindergarten, and strong programming in literacy, special education, and English Second Language services. These programs attracted students and families from outside our district. With the revenue limits, the only hope for a district to avoid severe cuts was to pass a referendum. In 2006, Fort Atkinson was one of only a few districts that passed a referendum.

If you were a winner in open-enrollment with more students coming in than leaving, the revenue stream was a real boost. Fort Atkinson was such a district, yet I felt sorry for our neighboring districts, who were losing, in some cases, millions of dollars in pupil revenue. I knew then the only way we would ever remain a winner in this open enrollment era was to pass operational referendums to exceed the revenue limits. In 2011, after the 2006 non-recurring referendum was ready to sunset, we went to the citizens again, this time requesting a three-year non-recuring operational referendum to exceed the revenue limits. With five-thousand votes cast, we won by four votes after a recount! When you hear the expression every vote counts!, believe it! Had we lost that vote, the cuts I had in my drawer would have been devastating to the learning community. The good Lord was looking out for me!

One of the lessons I learned was that Fort Atkinson citizens would not always give you exactly what you wanted, but they would come through in giving you what you needed! I could live with that, especially after seeing fellow superintendents lose one operational referendum after another.

A very devastating blow to public education in Wisconsin was the passage of Act 10, signed into law by Governor Walker on March 11th, 2011. This legislation (called the budget repair bill) was designed to defeat a projected 3.6 billion budget deficit for the 2011-2013 biennial budget. However, it was primarily aimed at teachers, ending most collective bargaining rights for public employee labor unions, exempting certain public safety unions such as police, fire fighters, and sheriff's deputies. This legislation polarized communities, and teachers were villainized unjustly. This legislation impacted salaries and benefits for teachers with yearly salary increases tied to the Consumer Price Index (CPI). The collateral damage from this act is still felt today as fewer young people in Wisconsin are seeking careers as teachers.

Our community was hit hard by Act 10. The relational trust we had established now rested with the school board. Unlike many school boards in Wisconsin, we maintained a respectful relationship with the faculty and staff. Somehow we got through this volatile period of time.

On the home front Therese after working in the Jefferson School District for seven years, got a call from a close friend in Beloit who taught French. She mentioned to Therese that her old Spanish job at Aldrich had opened up, and she hoped she would apply. Therese, while enjoying the students in Jefferson, never felt quite attached to that school district. She applied and was hired. Our son Mike was now out of high school, and our daughter Megan was working as a lobbyist for the American Dental hygienists.

Therese and I also purchased a modest lake home (a fix me up) on Little Green Lake in Markesan, Wisconsin, a little more than an hour away from Fort Atkinson. It would prove to be a nice place to retreat to on some weekends and in the summer. It also gave us an opportunity to hook up again with our dear friends Craig and Connie Ghinazzi, whom we first met during our Newman days when Craig and I were both on the faculty and coaching staff.

As I was approaching the age of sixty, I was looking forward to my next career step. I wanted to leave some time for teaching at the collegiate level in an Educational Administration Department. In October of 2012, I announced my plans to retire on June 30th of 2013 after fourteen years as Superintendent in Fort Atkinson. Overall, I had a really good run! A retirement reception at the high school in the afternoon, and later that evening, a dinner was held in my honor on St. Patrick's Day, Saturday, March 17th, 2013. Hundreds of people came to the open house reception. The dinner that night was held in a packed ballroom. I was surprised by how many people turned out that day and evening, expressing gratitude for my efforts. It was a wonderful send-off with some good spirited roasting and some very kind testimonials. The dinner served that night was corned beef, cabbage, and potatoes! How lucky could an Irishman get!

Summary Comments and leadership takeaways from this Chapter:

- You cannot lead unless you have earned relational trust. Once lost, you may never get it back.
- *The five key questions* when assuming a leadership position: People want you to value their thoughts and feelings.
- Honesty and candidness is expected of a leader.
- Bob Baxter (the taxpayer watchdog): As a leader, keeping your poise when your blood is boiling makes an impression on those around you.
- In times of tragedy and sorrow, step up and lead with compassion, but solicit an army to help you through the tough times.
- Never doubt your Faith or how strong it is, or the power of prayer, in your most challenging times.
- My first School Board in Fort Atkinson: Be grateful for people who have the confidence to take a chance on you, even when you are unproven, in stepping into a new role.
- Once again, a recurring theme of leadership: you can't do it alone. Trust and delegate to others in helping you reach the desired outcomes of your learning community or organization.

Part 3:
Giving Back

Epilogue

2013 TO PRESENT

Time to Pay it Forward and GIVE BACK!

As my final days as superintendent in Fort Atkinson approached in June of 2013, many teachers, administrators, staff, parents, and some high schoolers, would drop by my office to wish me well. On my last day, my office was pretty much cleared out, pictures removed, and all my belongings packed in boxes as the final hours of my fourteen-year tenure drew near. It sort of dawns on you in a surreal way, that this is really it! The last thing I did was to leave a hand-written note for my successor wishing him well and offering my assistance if he ever needed it.

While I had some melancholy feelings as I set my keys on the desk for the last time, I was excited for what the future might hold for me. Thinking back to 1997, I remembered how exciting it was to be on the UW campus. In fact, those feelings were the same as in the summer of 1977 when Father McClean had first encouraged me to enroll in the Master's program for principal certification at the University of Iowa!

The first item of business for Therese and me after my last day was to plan a summer vacation, which would be our first in thirteen years. Therese knew and planned just the right type of trip to get me to relax. We visited the NFL Hall of Fame, in Canton, Ohio, the MLB Hall of Fame, in Cooperstown, New York, and followed our Cubbies to games in Philadelphia and Toronto. It was a long driving vacation where we traveled through some beautiful parts of the country, especially in upstate New York, on our way to Cooperstown.

Megan and BJ wedding

Upon return, I got busy applying for faculty positions in Educational Leadership. I was really hoping something would open at UW-Madison. However, there were no openings. Then I got a call from Professor Dean Bowles, my UW-doctoral advisor. He was invited as a Fulbright Fellow to teach at a university in Latvia in the Fall of 2013. I filled in for him for a semester in an Admin course he was scheduled to teach. Some good experience, but only temporary, and I wasn't going to be satisfied as an adjunct professor, I wanted a full-time faculty position.

In the upcoming months, I was invited to interview at four universities. In the Summer of 2014, I was hired as a full-time professor at National Louis University (NLU) in Chicago, where I continue to work with aspiring school leaders desiring to become principals, superintendents, or central office administrators. I teach in both the Master's and Doctoral programs, along with providing supervision for internships and serving on dissertation committees.

I love teaching and have worked with almost a thousand candidates and still counting, as the Fall term of 2025 will soon be commencing. I published a book; *Beyond Theories and Degrees: The Alley Smarts of Educational Leadership 2020)*. I wrote the book in an effort to give back to the profession, in emulating the wonderful mentors I had throughout my career. Hopefully, the book has, and will continue to inspire candidates to take that next step into leadership. I am pleased that NLU and other colleges assign my book as required reading in some courses.

Mike, BJ, Megan, Therese, and me…beautiful wedding day

I think I learn as much from my students as they learn from me. I am not an academic or a scholar by any stretch of the imagination. I would describe myself as a grinder who, after forty-years of leadership as a principal and superintendent in Pre-K-12 schools, learned a few lessons along the way, that I can share with my students. Teaching theory is good, but teaching from experience is better. Integrity, using common sense, and being a good listener, will always help you in striving to do the right thing in leadership.

Mike looking sharp before wedding

Like Professors Chambers and Bowles, and all the great mentors who helped me along the way, I, too, want to pay it forward in GIVING BACK. That begins with my parents, Jim and Annamae Fitzpatrick, who raised us in a home where there was love, support, and a deep commitment to the Catholic Faith. I think of them every day, and I am still in awe of how they did it!

I still see those piercing blue eyes of little league coach Bill Neuman, telling me "get back in the box" -a great lesson to pass on to others that we need to stay focused and compartmentalize. Then there is Sister Carol, confronting meanness, and showing how outward kindness can really lift people.

So, as I come to the end of this book, I have gone full-circle. My Catholic Faith and career have intersected often throughout my life. With God's help, I got through the tough times while experiencing many triumphs. Thanks again, Mom and Dad, for providing the foundational values of faith, responsibility, and giving your best.

Therese giving a toast at the wedding

My seven siblings, whom I love dearly, and now their extended families! Mom would often refer to her children as the "Magnificent eight!" At one point in writing this book, I contemplated having each sibling write a chapter. However, what I realized was that their lens in growing up in our home was different than mine. Each of them have their own story to tell. However, the one endearing bond that we all share is the deep love and devotion for Mom and Dad, and the sacrifices they made for all of us. Our parents everlasting gift to us was an indestructible family spirit, in always being there for each other!

To the teachers and coaches who influenced me, and were so invested in me: Coach Pauls, Coach Hoppenstedt, Jim Walsh, Sister Carol, Coach Owen, and even Father "No Fun Dunne!"

My great early mentors when I began my teaching career- Father John McClean, Father Ken Gehling, who exercised such patience with young educators, while still conveying the high expectations educators must have for themselves in working with youth.

Bob Steele, my first public school boss, who taught me firsthand what governance in a public school looked like with the savvy he possessed, and Del Jeneary in West Liberty, who taught me to really appreciate the Arts in a school district.

To Fran Fruzen, a man I admire so much for the counsel and friendship he provided in helping me transition to a large school principalship. And to all the Purple Knights of Beloit!

The Board members, administrative team members, faculty, staff, and families of Fort Atkinson who helped me advance Fort Atkinson in becoming a beacon district in Wisconsin.

To my children, Megan and Mike. I am so proud of the people they have become, the challenges they conquered, and the goodness and kindness I see them extend to others. And my son-in-law BJ, and our two grandsons Jimmy and Paddy-who have enriched the lives of Therese and me in so many ways.

In closing, I owe my deepest love and gratitude to my wife Therese, who has been with me through thick and thin. I could never fully pay her back for the sacrifices she has made, so I could always take that next step forward in fulfilling my dreams. Her selflessness, is only exceeded by the love I have for her that knows no bounds!

This book could be entitled, *A Work of Thanksgiving*. God knows, I have been blessed!

Spring Training in Arizona with best friend Tim in middle and Marc Weisenburger

Meg and BJ with grandsons: Paddy on the left, Jimmy on the right

The Magnificent 8: as mom referred to us. Next to me on left are KK, Tony, Therese, Maryann, Annemarie, Jeannie, and Kevin. Sadly our beloved Tony passed away on October, 4 2025